"You're no gentleman, Brick, you're a beast," Helen said tartly.

His chuckle was wicked, and shivers skittered over her skin. "You were always good at taming beasts," he said. "Tame me, Helen."

"Let me go."

"Afraid?"

"No, I'm not scared of the devil."

"You should be," he murmured, and in one swift motion captured her lips. He was Sherman sweeping through Atlanta, Hannibal crossing the Alps, Tarzan swinging through the jungle with Jane. . . .

And she was swept off her feet. As soon as she could get her breath she was going to protest. Loudly. As soon as she found the energy she was going to clamp down on his lips with her teeth. As soon as the moon turned to green cheese she was going to stop kissing him back. Fast.

But for now she was in meltdown. He was gentle and fiery, poetic and passionate. What had started out as punishment had turned into exquisite torture. They were making love as only true lovers can.

"Tell me to stop," he whispered.

"No . . ."

WHAT ARE *LOVESWEPT* ROMANCES?

They are stories of true romance and touching emotion. We believe those two very important ingredients are constants in our highly sensual and very believable stories in the LOVESWEPT *line. Our goal is to give you, the reader, stories of consistently high quality that may sometimes make you laugh, sometimes make you cry, but are always fresh and creative and contain many delightful surprises within their pages.*

Most romance fans read an enormous number of books. Those they truly love, they keep. Others may be traded with friends and soon forgotten. We hope that each LOVE-SWEPT *romance will be a treasure—a "keeper." We will always try to publish*

LOVE STORIES YOU'LL NEVER FORGET
BY AUTHORS YOU'LL ALWAYS REMEMBER

The Editors

Loveswept®
727

CAN'T STOP LOVING YOU

PEGGY WEBB

BANTAM BOOKS
NEW YORK · TORONTO · LONDON · SYDNEY · AUCKLAND

CAN'T STOP LOVING YOU

A Bantam Book / February 1995

LOVESWEPT *and the wave design are registered trademarks of Bantam Books, a division of Bantam Doubleday Dell Publishing Group, Inc. Registered in U.S. Patent and Trademark Office and elsewhere.*

If you would be interested in receiving protective vinyl covers for your Loveswept books, please write to this address for information:

Loveswept
Bantam Books
P.O. Box 985
Hicksville, NY 11802

ISBN 0-553-44454-9

Published simultaneously in the United States and Canada

Bantam Books are published by Bantam Books, a division of Bantam Doubleday Dell Publishing Group, Inc. Its trademark, consisting of the words "Bantam Books" and the portrayal of a rooster, is Registered in U.S. Patent and Trademark Office and in other countries. Marca Registrada. Bantam Books, 1540 Broadway, New York, New York 10036.

PRINTED IN THE UNITED STATES OF AMERICA

OPM   0 9 8 7 6 5 4 3 2 1

This book is for Johnie Sue, for the many years of friendship and the many ways she has shown her love and loyalty.

"Where two raging fires meet together
They do consume the thing that
feeds their fury."

The Taming of the Shrew
SHAKESPEARE

AUTHOR'S NOTE

With this book, I never intended to veer away from the work of William Shakespeare, but that's exactly what I did. It wasn't my fault, really. My characters are responsible. From the moment I created Brick and Helen Sullivan, they took over.

"Wait a minute," I said when they took the stage in New Hampshire to reprise their roles in *The Taming of the Shrew.* "That's not Shakespeare."

"Be quiet and keep trying," they told me.

At first I wanted to argue with them, but having written thirtysomething novels and having been bossed around by my characters in every single one of them, I know that it's useless to argue. So I shut up and kept trying.

I'm glad I did. I only wish I'd thought first of what Brick and Helen Sullivan do to *The Taming of the Shrew.*

What a wonderful, mystical process writing is. In order to create characters that come alive, I have to be full of magic and dreams. Thank you, Tom, for bringing the magic and awakening the dreams.

And thank you, dear readers, for laughing with me and crying with me. But most of all, thank you for loving my stories and for writing to tell me so.

ONE

"Over my dead body!"

When Brick Sullivan got really mad, the furniture shook. The coffee table was doing a fandango across the wooden floor, the chandelier was rattling like an oak tree in a gale, and the stuffed pillows were cowering against the sofa like frightened rabbits.

Angelica Murphy tried to soothe her client.

"Now, Brick . . . this is not a firm commitment." He favored her with the lifted black brow and the curled lip that had earned him the adoration of fans around the world. "You know I would never make a commitment like that without consulting you. I *did*, however, give tentative approval to the plan, and I *strongly* urge you to consider it."

Brick paused in his thunderous stalking around her office, scooped the letter off her desk, and began to read aloud.

" 'This will surely be the event of the century: The reuniting of Sullivan and Sullivan in *The Taming of the Shrew.*' "

The voice that sent women swooning in the aisles of movie houses and theaters never failed to move Angelica to tears . . . of gratitude. If it weren't for Brick Sullivan, she would still be occupying a tiny little cubbyhole without a window instead of an office that commanded a view of Fifth Avenue.

Brick threw the letter back onto her desk.

"I've tamed that shrew once; I have no intention of ever doing it again. Onstage or off."

Knowing how Brick loved exits, she waited until he was at the door before having her say.

"Helen has already accepted."

He turned slowly, an actor from the top of his glorious mane of black hair to the tips of his polished number eleven boots. The brow went up once more.

"Obviously she doesn't know I'm part of the package."

"She knows."

"And she still accepted?"

"Of course. Your wife always did have great business sense."

"My ex."

"Sorry. I forgot."

"Like hell. You remember the make of socks I wore when I did my first Broadway show fifteen years ago. You never forget a damned thing, Angelica."

"Right."

"Wipe that witchy smile off your face. Hell will freeze over before I'll ever occupy the same stage as Helen Sullivan."

"You know what the gossip columnists will say. 'Brick Sullivan deserted his pet charity in a fashion worthy of the cowardly lion merely to avoid seeing the woman he loved on and off stage for five years. What does Helen Sullivan have that turns the mighty Brick into a sniveling mass of putty?' "

"I'll tell you what she has; she has claws."

"And a fabulous career that she's not willing to jeopardize over a simple matter of spending a few days in New Hampshire with you."

"I don't know why I put up with you. You exaggerate like hell."

"You put up with me because I'm gorgeous and sexy and I help you make more money than Ted Turner." Angelica's full-bodied chuckle caused her horn-rims to slide down her narrow nose and disturbed the starched front of her prim white blouse. "Ducking out of this small benefit performance will hardly jeopardize your career, Brick. But it will cast doubt on your commitment to the Children's Hospital."

Brick sank onto Angelica's plush sofa and crossed his long legs at the ankles.

"When do I start rehearsals?"

"How does tomorrow sound?"

"You didn't make a firm commitment, huh?"

"I knew you'd come around. Underneath all that rough-and-tumble bad-boy posturing, you're a teddy bear."

"Don't tell my fans."

Angelica trotted off to fetch a bottle of champagne from her break room. They always celebrated a deal with a toast: It was tradition for them. As Brick waited for her return, he began to lay his plans.

He hadn't seen Helen since their breakup two years earlier, and he harbored no doubts whatsoever about their first encounter. It would be all-out war, and he had no intention of going into battle without his armor.

Helen stood in front of the mirror practicing what she was going to say.

"Hello, Brick. How are you?"

No, that was too personal. She didn't want him to think she still cared how he was. And she certainly didn't want to *know*.

What if he'd weathered the two years better than she? What if he were gloriously happy and perfectly content in addition to being the most devastatingly gorgeous man she'd ever met?

She tossed her long black hair in the way that used to make him call her a high-bred filly and licked her full lower lip in the manner that used to drive him wild.

"Fancy seeing you again . . . after all these years."

That was better, spoken with just the right combination of nonchalance and bravado. Except that he would see right through the lie. Obviously she would never commit to do a show without knowing the other actors.

Tossing her hair and licking her lips was out too. She certainly didn't want him to think she was trying to seduce him. Even the Abominables were looking at her as if she had lost her mind.

She sank to the floor between her two Great Danes and wrapped her arms around their necks.

"What am I going to do, girls?"

Chelsea licked her face, and Sami licked her hand.

Helen giggled. "Well, yes, I suppose I could lick him all over, but he might get the wrong idea. Any other suggestions?"

"Talking to yourself again?" Marsha Jenkins, her personal secretary, marched into the bedroom and surveyed the damage like a general getting ready for war. A trail of silk lingerie led from the bureau to the open suitcase on the bed; shoes and handbags made a small lopsided mountain beside the chaise lounge; and jewelry glittered on the satin coverlet like fallen stars. "How many times have I told you to leave the packing to me?"

"At least a hundred."

"You're not even sorry for this mess." Pursing her lips, Marsha attacked the stack of lingerie as if it might fight back.

"I have not one speck of remorse. You'd be miserable if you didn't have a mess to straighten out."

"I'm miserable all the time anyhow." She favored Helen and the Danes with a mournful look, then proceeded to organize the shoes and handbags. "And I can't see how swapping this sweet Georgia winter for that drafty old barn Farnsworth calls a mansion is going to help my feelings one little bit. I've made up my mind; I'm not going."

"I'm taking everybody on this place, and that includes you, so you might as well unmake your mind."

"What in the devil do you need all of us for . . . as if I had to ask?"

"I don't intend for Brick Sullivan to be able to get within ten feet of me. He's lethal, and I'm taking no chances."

"*Love.*" Marsha's loud, disdainful snort told exactly what she thought of that matter. She scooped jewelry off the bed and marched toward Helen's dressing table, dripping ropes of pearls and diamonds. "If you'd consulted me in the first place, we wouldn't all be fixing to freeze our buns off way up yonder at the backside of nowhere."

Helen began to laugh.

"What's so funny?"

"Here I was, worried about how to keep Brick Sullivan at a respectable distance when I had the perfect weapon all along."

"I'm not even going to ask what."

"Just keep scowling. That face is enough to quell even the indomitable Brick." Helen gave her secretary an affectionate hug. "Is there anything else I can do to keep your ire up for the duration of this trip?"

"You'll think up plenty without me having to tell you."

Helen relaxed for the first time since she'd agreed to do a benefit with her ex-husband.

Philanthropist Milton Farnsworth didn't merely own a vast estate and the surrounding village; he owned the whole island. Plunked in the middle of Lake Winnipesaukee and set back among towering trees, Farnsworth Manor was a place a man could get lost in, and that was exactly what Brick Sullivan intended to do . . . after his first performance.

With his feet planted wide apart in the familiar devil-may-care stance, he surveyed his home for the next few weeks. Farnsworth had spared no expenses. Nor had he bothered with understated elegance. Everything about the house and grounds screamed *excess*, from the ornate Corinthian porticos to the stone gargoyles that guarded the front door.

Clouds hovering over the lake carried a promise of rain, and the chill breezes carried more than a hint of the snows that would soon come. Good weather for cuddling beside Farnsworth's giant stone fireplace . . . if he had the right woman.

"Brick baby, are you out here?"

The sound of Barb Gladly's voice made Brick think of fingernails being scraped across a chalkboard. She was definitely not the right woman, but she'd have to do for the next few weeks.

"I'm here," he said.

Everything about her bounced as she walked toward him, and he wondered if perhaps he hadn't overdone it a bit. Helen's appeal lay in the air of mystery that surrounded her. There was nothing remotely mysterious about Barb. All her assets were on prominent display. He hoped Helen wouldn't be suspicious.

"The hell with her," he muttered as Barb slithered to his side and wrapped herself around him.

"With me, Brick?"

"Not you."

"Helen?"

"Yes."

"When's she coming?"

"Any minute now. Are you ready?"

"I've been ready since I was born, baby."

"That's my girl." He pulled Barb close. "Let her come."

Helen Sullivan had never missed a cue. The

long white limousine pulled into the driveway. It was as if Helen had been waiting offstage to make her entrance.

The chauffeur opened her door, and the first thing Brick saw was the long, glorious legs of Helen Sullivan. He was totally unprepared for the sight. He had expected to feel the rage that filled him, but not the desire, not the quick, hot passion that settled into his loins like live coals.

He tightened his hold on Barb.

"Ready?" His voice was rough and raw with emotion.

"Anytime, baby."

He waited until Helen was out of the car before he started kissing Barb. It was a stage kiss, designed so he never lost contact with the audience.

His *audience* was standing facing the portico now, the wind blowing her skirt against her legs and lifting her dark gypsy hair away from her face. He'd never been able to look at her and remain unmoved. That hadn't changed. His groin tightened almost painfully, and his breath came in labored spurts.

"Hmmm, good, baby," Barb murmured, pressing closer.

"Don't overdo it," he said.

"I can't help myself."

At least Barb was honest. At least she hadn't taken his ring and his name and his heart and then walked out the door.

Not one flicker of emotion crossed Helen's face as she watched them kiss.

Damn her soul to black everlasting hell.

She turned back to the limousine, and out barreled the Abominables. They'd been mere puppies when Brick had given them to her for her birthday three years earlier, but they were nearly as big as Shetland ponies now.

Brick loved her for keeping the dogs and hated her for depriving him of seeing them grow up. Chelsea and Sami. Named for his grandmother and hers in much the same way ordinary people named their children.

Next came the cat. Gwenella used to hide behind the curtains and pounce on their bed right in the midst of their most amorous moments. Helen always laughed when Brick threatened to banish the Persian from the bedroom.

"Look at that self-satisfied smirk of hers. She knows you're a big softie, darling. Besides, you would never deprive her of her entrance."

The cat had stayed. Because Gwenella didn't like water, the bathroom became their playground.

The sound of water lapping against the shore triggered memories that stoked the fires of Brick's fury. He escalated the kiss, all the while keeping an eye on Helen Sullivan and her entourage.

She'd kept the same secretary and the same personal fitness trainer. Brick was pleased, though he didn't dare analyze his secret glee.

Bundled up as if she were attempting an expedition to the North Pole, Marsha issued orders that everybody except Helen obeyed. Instead Helen stood by the car, laughing while her tiny, indomitable secretary got the crew moving in not too orderly a fashion.

Gwenella sassed Chelsea, who retreated in alarm and wrapped her leash around the trainer's legs. With a mountain of Great Dane pulling at him, Matt Rider might have gone down if he hadn't had muscles the size of Arkansas. As it was, he merely unwrapped the first dog only to have the second try to hide between his legs when the cat took exception to something Sami had done.

Helen moved in the midst of the melee, laughing in her throaty way and flashing her dark eyes in his direction.

Brick wanted to catch her by the shoulders and shake her until her teeth rattled. Then he wanted to throw her over his shoulder and disappear into the woods until he had loved the truth out of her.

Why did you leave me, Helen?

It was Chelsea who started the entire crew moving in his direction. With a yelp that sounded like recognition, she broke loose from Matt and raced across the portico, her long tongue hanging out in the goofy smile he remembered and her tail flapping like a flag in a windstorm.

Suddenly Brick had his audience.

"Hello, Brick."

That was all Helen said. Just *hello* and then his

name, all soft and sexy the way she used to say it when the lights were low and the fire was crackling and he was stroking her long, long legs.

"Helen." Lord, he sounded like a dying calf in a hailstorm. He'd have to do better than that if he wanted to survive the next two weeks with Helen Sullivan. "I see you still travel light."

Several of Farnsworth's employees had come from the house and were struggling up the steps under the weight of her luggage. She stood amidst her entourage as bright as the evening star in a New Hampshire sky, and just as inaccessible.

"I travel with the people and the possessions that are necessary to me."

"So do I." With a subtle pressure of his arm, he positioned Barb for the best effect. Her blatant sexual impact was totally lost on Helen, but Matt got pink around the ears. "Helen, meet my fiancée, Barb Gladly."

"Nice to meet you, Barb. Congratulations," Helen said, her eyes never leaving his face.

He'd expected more of a reaction. He decided to goad until he got one.

"You used to have more than that to say in the shower."

"You used to put on a better show in the shower."

The gleam in her eye told him he'd scored. That and the color in her cheeks. He bit back his gloating grin.

"This scene on the portico has all the makings of a grade B movie," she added.

"Even grade B movies have appreciative audiences."

As if she'd heard her cue, Chelsea licked his hand and, for good measure, licked his shoes.

Helen chuckled. "You know how Chelsea is. She never could resist a good ham."

With that parting shot, she swept toward the front door.

"Did I do all right?" Barb asked after Helen had disappeared into the house.

"You were great. Thanks."

"Is it all right if I take a walk? I'd like to get a good look at this place."

"Do whatever you like. Just be sure to be at dinner on time, dressed to kill."

Catching her lower lip between her front teeth, Barb glanced toward the front door, obviously awestruck.

"I can't believe I was that close to Helen Sullivan," she said.

"Neither can I."

The smell of Helen's perfume still lingered on the portico. He didn't dare breathe deeply until he was safely in the woods.

Thinking of the next few days with her made his stomach turn over. He hadn't won the first skirmish, but he'd survived. He could do it again.

TWO

"Are you unpacking these clothes or mutilating them?"

In a fine fury, Helen threw the plain gray slacks in the general direction of the closet and whirled toward Marsha.

"Did you see the size of those"—Helen gestured dramatically toward her own small breasts—"*things?* Like the peaks of Mt. Rushmore. And that fanny. I'll lay you odds it was hip pads."

She stalked across the room, trailing classic white blouses. The Abominables hid their faces behind their paws, and even the audacious Gwenella scooted out of the way.

"Fiancée, indeed!" She kicked a pair of black riding boots on her march back to the suitcase. "I'll bet she's after his money . . . or his you know what."

"No. What?" The doleful Marsha had a wicked side.

"I'm going to fire you, Marsha."

"You already did. Twice today."

"Well, I'm going to mean it next time."

"Who in the world would put up with you?"

Helen sank to the floor and wrapped her hands around her knees. With her bare feet and freshly scrubbed face she looked more like a teenager than a famous star of stage and screen.

Marsha had a hard time retaining her stern demeanor. It wouldn't do for both of them to get sentimental at the same time.

"She really was quite winsome, wasn't she, Marsha?"

"I offer no opinion. Obviously Brick likes her, and that's all that counts."

"Ouch."

Marsha put her hands on her hips and stretched her neck the way she always did when she was getting ready to deliver a lecture.

"Now you listen to me, missy. I don't know why in the world you ever left the man in the first place, and I don't want to know. But the fact is, you did. And now he's got another woman." Leaning down, she shook a bony finger in Helen's face. "I'm not fixing to watch you make a fool of yourself. You put on your glad rags and hold your head up as if you're *somebody.*"

Helen stood up, five inches taller than Marsha even in her bare feet.

"I'm Helen Sullivan, actress."

"Then, by george, *act.*"

Helen kissed her cheek. "You're not fired any-more, Marsha."

"I never was in the first place."

Jealousy was not her motive. At least that's what Helen told herself as she slithered down the staircase like the serpent in the Garden of Eden.

Her red Chinese dress fit like sin. Each step she took revealed a long length of silk-clad leg.

"My dear, you look smashing."

Her host came to the foot of the staircase and gazed raptly up at her. But Farnsworth was not her target. Her target was leaning casually against the mantel, lifting his famous sardonic eyebrow at her as if to say, "I know exactly what you're up to."

She wasn't even sure herself what she was up to. Maybe she wanted to prove that she could act any part in any situation, including *ex-wife meets husband's fiancée and emerges triumphant.*

Farnsworth escorted her into the enormous paneled room and placed her in a seat of honor beside the hearth. A chilled drink was handed to her, and she made small talk with her host until he trotted off to show his gun collection to Matt Rider and Barb Gladly.

Brick's eyes blazed like the fires of hell as he started toward her, every move calculated. Riveted, she watched him come. Shivers skittered down her spine, and hairs along the back of her neck stood on end. She only hoped that the heat flushing her body didn't show in her face.

"It won't work."

His voice was smoky and intimate, for her ears only. He towered over her, deliberately position-ing himself so that she was eye level with his crotch. If she'd had a gun, she would have shot him.

She had to wet her dry lips with her tongue before she was capable of speech.

"What won't work?"

"That Maggie the Cat role you're playing."

Maggie the Cat, who tried every ploy in the book to get her husband's attention. Come to think of it, she felt rather like a cat on a hot tin roof.

"I'm not playing a role. I'm dressed for din-ner."

"You're dressed for seduction." Brick leaned down and casually ran one finger around the high collar of her dress, skimming the sensitive skin of her throat. "I bought the dress for you in New Orleans, then took it off of you in the Hotel Saint Helene."

It had been a night to remember. They'd both said the dress would always remind them of that night.

His hand left her throat, but he might as well have been stripping her bare in the presence of Farnsworth's dinner guests. The front of her dress rose and fell in telltale agitation.

"Do you remember, Helen?"

Silently she damned the wicked impulse that had sent her slithering down the stairs in her red dress.

His slow, audacious gaze raked her face and the front of her dress.

"No need to answer that," he said. "I can see that you do."

"Damn you, Brick Sullivan."

"You disappoint me, Helen. An actress with no better line than that. Come, my darling. Surely you can think of something better."

"You're the one with all the lines tonight . . . and all the moves too. Why should I upstage you?"

"You've done it before."

"Yes, and I'll do it again."

"But not tonight, my sweet. In spite of that sinfully seductive dress and those long, silky legs, you will play only a minor role. Brick Sullivan has a new leading lady."

". . . whose charms are obvious."

"Not all of them, my love."

Helen bared her claws.

"She has something I haven't seen?" Her sweet smile belied her words.

"Yes . . . Loyalty."

She sucked in an angry breath. Brick pinned her to the seat with his fierce black eyes, daring her to refute him.

What do you know about loyalty? she wanted to

scream. *What do you know about being abandoned?*
But of course she couldn't say those things to him,
not when they were in a room full of people.

Not now. Not ever.

"How lovely for both of you," she said. Her
voice was firm, cheerful, a masterpiece of control.
She could have commented that Miss Loyalty was
at that moment wrapped around Matt Rider's
muscled arm, but she saw no need to truly earn
the nickname Maggie the Cat.

Brick held her with his eyes a heartbeat longer,
his lips parted as if he had something else to say;
but in the end he left her. Abruptly. The master of
the dramatic exit left without the last word, and
Helen finally understood the depth of his turmoil.

In that instant she knew nostalgia and something sharper, something much deeper. Helen
knew regret.

How he had survived dinner, Brick would
never know. During this trip he was destined to
do his best acting offstage.

He paced his room in the south wing like a
novice backstage at his first performance. The
thick carpet muffled his footsteps, and the heavy
drapery muffled his curses.

Helen's red dress had been lethal. It had taken
all his willpower to keep his eyes off her.

He needed cold air . . . and lots of it. Ripping off his tie and flinging aside his dinner jacket, he grabbed his parka and headed outside.

Helen considered it a miracle that she had survived dinner. Her hands shook as she unzipped her red dress and stepped into a pair of jeans and a sweatshirt.

When Brick had draped his arm around Barb's shoulders, she'd wanted to kill them both. And that was just for starters.

By the time dessert was served Helen had been ready to string them up by the heels, cover them with honey, and hang them outside for the bears to eat.

Were there bears in New Hampshire? She had no earthly idea. If there were, she was going to take her chances.

One more minute in the Farnsworth mansion with Brick Sullivan just down the hall was going to drive her over the brink.

She grabbed her cozy anorak and headed for the great outdoors.

The golf course was a mysterious landscape of moonlight and shadows. Brick walked mostly in the shadows, for the darkness suited his mood. With his fists clenched at his sides, he took deep breaths, trying to get Helen out of his system.

It was an impossible task. She still smoked through him, a fire that refused to be smothered.

Icy winds whipped his open jacket back from his body. He was dressed for a stroll down a Georgia lane, not a stalk through the New Hampshire night in the dead of winter. He'd probably freeze to death.

Which might be an improvement over his present state.

A night bird called from the nearby forest, mocking him. If he had any sense at all, he wouldn't even be out here; he'd be cozied up next to Barb in her warm bed.

She'd invited him.

Not only was he playing a besotted fool where Helen was concerned, but he was a besotted fool with a code of honor, warped though it might be. He never used women. Barb was being paid handsomely for a job, and that job did not include sleeping with the boss.

Beset by demons, he pulled his collar up, rammed his hands into his pockets, and forged on, occasionally kicking at the tight turf as if stones were blocking his path. Suddenly the back of his neck prickled, and he was aware that he was not alone.

Stopping in the shadows, he lifted his head and strained his eyes into the darkness. She was there on the seventh green, her silhouette as unmistakable as if she'd been standing under the bright lights of a stage instead of in the pale, cold light of the moon.

Brick clenched his hands into fists. Helen Sullivan on the seventh green. Had the same memories that brought him there sent her winging into the night?

Rage tightened his jaw, and hard on its heels came a sense of loss so painful, he almost cried aloud.

Memories overwhelmed him. . . .

She'd been in one of her kittenish, playful moods that night. The gold glitter in the center of her green eyes always tipped him off.

He set his bags inside the door, happy to be home from a three-month tour of Much Ado About Nothing, *but happier still to be facing the woman he'd dreamed about every blessed sleepless night and longed for every waking moment.*

"Come here, wench. Your lord and master is home."

"Not until I finish basting the beast, darling. The way to a man's heart, they say . . ." With a wicked grin she cast aside the dark green terry cloth robe she was wearing and stood before him in heels and a flirty blue apron—and not a stitch more.*

He stood beside the door, raking his eyes over her, loving the way she responded, the quick tightening of her nipples, the tiny shivers that rippled along her skin, the way she licked her full bottom lip.

Neither of them moved. Both of them knew how

much better the loving would be when it was honed to a fine edge by anticipation.

"You baked a beast for me? You, the woman who abhors the kitchen?"

"Every now and then I'm willing to make the supreme sacrifice to satisfy your ravenous appetite."

"There's only one thing that will satisfy my appetite tonight."

"Don't tell me. Let me guess."

Ever aware of her audience, she put a finger to her temple in a saucy way that lifted her breasts. The heat coursing along his veins turned to a full-fledged firestorm.

"Strawberries," she said, grinning at him. "In strategic places."

"How strategic?"

"Very."

Her tongue slid over her bottom lip once more, then rested there, teasing him. He took one step toward her, then another . . . and another, his eyes never leaving that sexy pink tongue.

"Can I have all I want, Helen?"

"How much do you want?"

"About two quarts."

"Only two? I thought you said you were ravenous."

"That's for starters." He stood before her now, so awed by the perfection of her body that he hardly knew which part of her to touch first. With one finger he traced her damp bottom lip, then trailed it down the side of her throat and across the swell of her right breast.

"For starters?" she asked, her breath already hitching in her throat.

"I thought we'd have a little exercise before we eat."

"Anything in particular in mind?"

"Golf."

"In the dark?"

"I play my best game in the dark."

She slid one finger into the small gap between the third and fourth buttons on his shirt and began to draw hot, erotic circles. That tiny contact of flesh against flesh was almost enough to make him lose control.

"Show me," she said.

With slow deliberation he put his hands on her shoulders and turned her around. The long, slender length of her body from neck to ankle was bisected by the perky bow of her apron. He skimmed his palms down her back, loving the way she shivered, loving the way her skin was already heated.

He untied the bow, and the wisp of an apron drifted to the floor. Helen lifted her hair off her neck with one hand then turned toward him.

"I'm afraid I have nothing to wear for this game."

"Nothing is exactly what I had in mind."

She reached for his belt buckle, and suddenly the waiting became too much for both of them. Buttons ripped, the metal buckle clanged against the floor, his pants bounced off the bar and landed on a chair.

Then she was in his arms, and he was racing through the French doors. A nip of fall was in the air, *and when the night breezes swept over them, their skin tightened like the peel of a crisp, juicy apple.*

The seventh green lay before them, shadowed by a copse of oak trees, the gentle swell of earth spread out blanketlike and inviting. He was in her before they touched the ground.

The feel of her around him made his senses reel.

"No more road tours," he said, meaning it.

"Liar."

She pushed him back against the cold, prickly grass; then, poised above him like some fine racing filly from Kentucky, she made him forget that he'd said the same thing dozens of times before and that she knew he would always change his mind.

And she didn't care. Acting was in his blood . . . and hers.

They would always be on the road, living out of a suitcase and keeping the telephone hot, moving so fast that the cities soon ran together and nothing was real except the bright lights of the stage and the one who waited at home.

Wind rattled the dead leaves of the oak trees and bit at their naked flesh, but nothing could stop the momentum that sent them reeling over the ground, sometimes racing along like two thoroughbreds in a dead heat, sometimes pausing to touch and taste, to explore and savor.

And when at last their passion was sated, she bent over him with her hair cascading over his belly and licked the fine sheen of perspiration caught in the valley over his heart.

"Promise," she whispered.

"Anything," he said, meaning that too.

"Promise we'll never lose the spontaneity."

"Never, Helen. As long as I have breath in my body."

It was a promise he was destined to break. Not because he wanted to but because two years later she'd walked out the door and never came back.

Now she was standing on another golf course in another state with her face lifted in pensive attitude toward the moon as if she, too, remembered and, remembering, felt the keen sense of loss and the hopeless sense that everything that should have been perfect, that *was* perfect, had somehow slipped through their grasp. Helen and Brick Sullivan, the two most successful Shakespearean actors of their time, couldn't make the thing most important to them work: Their marriage.

"Damn you to hell, Helen."

The wind caught his whisper and carried it up to the treetops where it startled an owl, who lifted his wings and soared into the darkness. Helen turned slowly in his direction.

"Who's there?" she asked. He stood quietly, not wanting to be discovered—especially by Helen, especially near the seventh green. Her hand, glowing white in the moonlight, flew to her throat. "Is someone there?"

Damned his warped code of honor. He couldn't bear to frighten her. He stepped out of the shadows.

"It's only me, Helen."

"Brick."

Was that panic he heard in her voice . . . or longing?

"I didn't mean to scare you."

"I wasn't scared, just startled."

She lifted her hair off her neck in an unconsciously seductive gesture. Or perhaps it was calculated. He didn't know Helen anymore, hadn't known her since she'd left him.

In order to keep his thoughts from taking dangerous dips and turns, he studied her. She was no more dressed for walking in a cold New Hampshire night than he. Her sweatshirt was cotton, and her anorak was much too lightweight to do more than break the wind.

In the old days he'd have offered her his coat, then wrapped his arms around her so his body heat would warm her.

The old days were dead. He had to keep reminding himself of that fact.

"You picked a strange time to go walking, Helen. Was an evening in my company that disturbing for you?"

He hoped it was. He wanted to see her suffer.

"How like you to take credit for everything, Brick. My walk has nothing whatsoever to do with you."

"That's good to know. I wouldn't want us to start rehearsals with any misunderstandings between us."

"You've made your position perfectly clear, and now I'll state mine. Miss Thirty-eight, twenty-six, thirty-eight can have you. I'm clearly not interested."

"Clearly."

He cast a significant glance at their surroundings. For a moment the unflappable Helen was flustered, then she quickly recovered her composure.

"I don't know what you're thinking . . ."

"You don't?" Full of memories and unable to help himself, he caught her wrists in a tight grip. "You never could lie well, Helen."

"No, I never could lie well."

With her chin tilted at a stubborn angle and her eyes sparking fire, she challenged him.

"You remember . . ."

"Don't." She jerked out of his grasp. "I remember every detail, including the way you taste. But that doesn't mean I want to taste you again."

He tried to hide his wounded male pride as well as his disappointment, though what he had to be disappointed about was beyond him. Hadn't he hired Barb Gladly for the specific purpose of keeping Helen at a distance?

"First the red dress, then the seventh green. You could have fooled me, Helen."

"You always did have an overactive imagination, Brick. I suggest you put it to good use studying your lines."

In the regal manner that had captivated fans

the world 'round, Helen Sullivan left him standing on the golf course with nothing but the cold
wind for company. The moon glinted on her hair
and reflected off the pale silk of her anorak. When
she turned toward the house, it illuminated her
profile, face, and body, which were every bit as
perfect as he remembered.

Rocking back on his heels, he stuffed his hands
into his pockets.

"I'd rather study *your* lines, Helen," he said.

When she disappeared into the house, he
shook himself. Helen Sullivan was a witch. He'd
fallen under her spell once; he had no intention of
doing it again.

Ever.

"Then what am I doing standing out here
freezing my butt off?"

Brick hastened to the house and mounted the
stairs two at a time. When he strode past Helen's
door, he didn't even glance to see if her light was
on.

In his room he got out his script and perused
the familiar lines. As he read he began to grin.

Tomorrow Helen Sullivan would rue the day
she ever agreed to share a stage with her ex-husband.

THREE

Helen told herself she was ready for rehearsals with her ex-husband. She had her entire crew backstage. Matt and the animals were stationed near the curtain so they could see all the action, and Marsha was stationed at her elbow. Brick would easily get past the Abominables, but he would never make it beyond Matt Rider, and if he did, he wouldn't get past Marsha.

Of course, he'd made it perfectly clear he didn't *want* to get past anybody, but that small fact did nothing to calm her.

"Act two, scene one!" the director called. "We'll take it from Katharina's entrance."

"He did that deliberately," she said, turning toward her secretary.

"Who?" Marsha held out a glass of water with a slice of lemon.

"Brick. He's been over there for the last thirty minutes plotting with the director."

"What's wrong with act two, scene one?"

Instead of answering, Helen narrowed her eyes in the direction of her ex-husband.

"If he thinks he's going to intimidate me, he has another think coming."

With that parting shot she tossed back her hair and marched onto the stage.

Marsha joined Matt near the curtain.

"Looks as if there's a storm brewing," she said.

"It's long overdue," he said.

Brick knew that look of Helen's, that walk, that stubborn chin. Adrenaline pumped through him. He felt exhilarated, challenged, ready for battle.

He watched through lowered lids as she took the opposite side of the stage.

"What's the matter, Helen? Afraid of this scene?"

"No. Nor any other scene in this play." He could feel the sparks as she marched across the stage and faced him nose to nose. "You might as well get this straight right from the beginning, Brick Sullivan. Anything that takes place on this stage is strictly a part of the theater. Including the sizzling kiss in act two, scene one."

"You've thought about it, have you?"

"Not at all. I just happen to know my Shakespeare."

"Places!" the director called.

Brick snaked his arm around Helen's waist as she turned to leave.

"Ready to be wooed, wildcat?"

She whirled on him.

"If you make one more move that's not in this script, you'll feel more than the sting of my tongue."

"I've felt it all before, Helen."

Her color came up. Mesmerized, he kept a tight grip on her waist.

They struck sparks off each other that could be seen even at the back of the auditorium where Barb Gladly was stationed.

"Hmmm," she said, drumming her long red fingernails on the top of her purse. When Brick finally let Helen go, Barb slid from her seat unnoticed and quietly made her way backstage. She had seen things that threw a whole new light on the carefully laid plans of Brick Sullivan.

Barb Gladly was nobody's fool. And besides that, she was the world's biggest romantic.

"It's time to make a few plans of my own." She knew just the person who would help her. Grinning like a cat in a cream factory, she headed straight to Matt Rider.

Clifford Oates had directed some of the finest Shakespearean actors in modern times, but he had never directed a pair as charismatic as Brick and

Helen Sullivan. They were virtual giants on the stage, filling it with a presence that almost overwhelmed an audience.

Sitting on the front row watching Helen take her place, Clifford felt the skin along the back of his neck prickle.

Helen didn't merely *act* Katharina; she *became* Katharina. She was fire and suppressed sexuality as she made her entrance.

Brick's Petruchio was arrogant, bold, and outrageous as he watched his ex-wife make her way toward him.

Clifford leaned forward in his seat. Something was happening onstage that was not due to mere presence, something electric, something magical. The voices of the great actors filled the room. By the time they got to lines that earned Shakespeare the reputation of being a bawdy bard, Clifford had almost forgotten that his job was to direct.

He had become a captive audience.

" 'Come, come, you wasp, i'faith, you are too angry.' "

As he spoke Petruchio's lines, Brick moved so close to Helen that his thigh touched hers. She didn't acknowledge by so much as a blink of the eye that he had done anything except what the script called for.

" 'If I be waspish, best beware my sting,' " she said.

There was the reaction he'd hoped for. It was in her voice, that high, bright edge that meant he'd disturbed her.

He pressed his advantage, moving closer still, so close, he felt the stiffening in her spine.

" 'My remedy is then, to pluck it out.' "

Ever the consummate professional, she didn't miss a cue.

" 'Ay, if the fool could find it where it lies.' " Her eyes warned him not to try.

" 'Who knows not where a wasp doth wear his sting? In his tail.' "

Boldly Brick snaked his arm behind her back and firmly planted his hand on her backside.

She stiffened as if she'd been shot. Giving him a scathing look, she marched to the proscenium and leaned toward the director.

"That's not in the script," she said.

Clifford roused himself like a man who had been drugged.

"It looked good to me," he said. "Natural."

"I don't care how it looked. It's not in the script. This is Shakespeare, not the Playboy channel."

"Brick and I discussed this before rehearsals . . ."

Helen whirled toward her ex-husband. "I'll just bet you did."

Brick sauntered toward her, walking in that maddening way he always used when he wanted to placate her. Instead of placating, his arrogance only fed her flame.

"Don't you take another step, Brick Sullivan."

"I'm the other star in this production, Helen. Any major dispute regarding stage directions will be overseen by me."

"This is not about stage directions; it's about mutiny."

Brick grinned. "Whose? Yours or mine?"

"Mine. I'm walking if you don't stick to the script." She placed her hands on her hips. "And it does not call for you to maul my butt."

"What makes you think I'd want to do a thing like that, Helen?"

His innocent posture enraged her. She stamped down on his foot. Ever the actor, Brick pretended more pain than he felt.

"Helen, why would you want to go and do a thing like that?"

"Because you deserve it, you wretched cad."

Clifford saw his entire production unraveling before his eyes. He hurried from his seat and joined them onstage. Placing one hand on Helen's arm and the other on Brick's, he mediated.

"Now, Brick . . . Helen. I know this is your first time onstage together in a while."

"Two years," she said.

"Two and a half," he said.

"Two."

"You left in April."

"It was August."

"I know because the forsythia was in bloom."

"It wasn't forsythia; it was marigolds."

Clifford had the sinking feeling that he was on a runaway train headed straight for the ravine of failed directors.

"Why don't we all take a break?" he said.

His suggestion was met with a hoot of laughter from Brick and a smile of derision from Helen.

"Who needs a break," Brick said. "This is merely a professional argument."

"Strictly professional," Helen agreed.

Clifford swallowed hard. "All right. Then let's start at the top of that scene."

"No need to waste time." Brick sauntered back to his place. "Let's just take it from where we left off."

"Good." Clifford took his seat once more, thinking that there was nothing good about it. "Now, where were we?"

"I had just discovered the stinger in her tail."

"Discovery, my foot." Helen crossed her arms and glared at him. "It was more like an invasion."

"Was it, now?" Brick stalked her, his voice silky and deadly. "An invasion, you say? That can be arranged."

"Not in this lifetime, Brick Sullivan."

Clifford smote his forehead. "I'm getting too old for this," he muttered.

In the wings, Marsha whispered to Matt, "What did I tell you?"

"It's better than I expected," he said. "Those

two are still madly in love." He winked at Barb Gladly, who had her arms wrapped around the necks of the Abominables.

"If they get any madder, they're going to kill each other." Marsha grabbed a glass of water, threw in a slice of lemon, and marched onstage.

"Break time," she announced.

Clifford groaned. *Now* he was taking directions from Godzilla the secretary.

Helen took a long, slow drink from the glass. The more she looked at Brick's maddeningly insolent smile, the madder she got. With careful deliberation she upended the glass over his head. Water drenched his hair, ice cubes slid into the neck of his shirt, and the wedge of lemon landed in the crook of his ear.

Dead silence filled the rehearsal hall. Brick and Helen stared at each other as if they were two gladiators prepared to fight to the death. Then suddenly Brick laughed. His hearty roar broke the tension, and soon everybody was chuckling and patting each other on the back and making their way to the break room for a fortifying cup of coffee.

"How do you want yours, Mr. Oates?" the girl at the coffee pot asked. "Cream? Sugar?"

"With a little TNT," the director said. "They say the only way to control a raging fire is to apply a little dynamite."

❖──────────❖

Break time did wonders to cool hot tempers. Or so Clifford thought.

They had started all over with act 2, scene 1, and Helen and Brick were sailing through their lines. Just as the director sank back into his chair and was starting to relax, they came to the deadly scene that had lately resulted in Helen cooling Brick off with a glass of ice water over his head.

" 'Who knows not where a wasp doth wear his sting? In his tail.' "

Clifford breathed a sigh of relief. This time Brick was being good. No hands on Helen's backside.

" 'In his tongue,' " she replied, every bit of Kate's tartness evident in her voice and her stance.

"Good . . . good," Clifford said.

He bragged too soon.

" 'Whose tongue?' " Brick's line. Spoken with a dangerous glint in his eye.

" 'Yours, if you talk of tails; and so farewell.' "

" 'What, with my tongue in your tail? nay, Good Kate; I am a gentleman'—"

Suddenly Brick caught Helen around the waist, sank onto a low bench, and tipped her over his lap.

Her roar of outrage filled the stage. She came out of his grasp flailing and kicking.

" 'That I'll try.' " Her line was served up with a stinging wallop that clipped Brick's jaw and knocked him backward across the bench.

"Cut . . . cut . . ." Clifford yelled.

Offstage the Abominables broke loose from Matt and galloped onto the stage. Straddling Brick, they licked his face, his ears, his hands.

Helen tugged at their leashes, trying to get them under control.

"Stop it," she said.

"Don't stop them. I'm a dying man."

"You're a conniving man. Get up off that floor."

"No. I want to lie here and wallow in my pain."

"You want to lie there and gloat in your victory. You meant to cause mayhem, and you did."

Helen did some fancy sidestepping to keep from getting tangled in the dog leashes.

"Now stop that," she said to her pets.

But they would have none of her commands. Giddy with joy, they gave their former master a tongue bath that showed *they* at least were delighted with the game he was playing.

The combined weight of the Great Danes was too much for Helen to handle. She went down in a heap, landing sprawled on top of Brick with her face merely inches from his.

"You insufferable rake," she said. "You blackguard. You . . . you . . ."

Helen sputtered to a stop, trapped not by anger but by emotions much deeper, much more disturbing. The gleam in Brick's dark eyes was the one she'd seen so many times before, the unmistakable gleam of passion . . . and the feelings that coursed through her were the unmistakable ones of response.

It had been so long. Two years. Two years without the quick, hot flash of desire, the endless delight, the joy of rushing into the arms of a man she had loved more than life itself.

Had loved, she kept reminding herself. She no longer loved Brick Sullivan. Couldn't afford to love him. Wouldn't let herself love him.

His eyes were black and deep and lit from the inside by the glow that had been only for her. Her lips trembled.

Lord, don't let me cry. Not here. Not now.

"Helen."

His whisper stirred the hair at her temple as he reached to touch her cheek.

"Helen."

Again, he whispered her name. There was wonder in his voice, wonder and a terrible pain. She closed her eyes, allowing herself the small forbidden luxury of his touch. His touch was light, exquisite, the stuff of dreams. His fingertips skimmed across her cheekbones, down the side of her throat, then back up to her lips.

A small tear slid from underneath her eyelid, unaware. She heard his quick intake of breath, felt the tremble in his hand.

His body was long and lean and hard, perfectly fitted to hers. They had always said so. Late at night cuddled together in the middle of their curtained bed, they used to marvel at their perfect fit, marvel and laugh, then love again just to be sure they hadn't been mistaken.

How beautiful their love had been, how magical, that combination of love and laughter that lingered in the heart and spirit and soul even when they were separated, that wonderous bonding destined by fate and smiled upon by the gods.

Brick slipped his finger between her lips and brushed lightly against the moist, satiny inner lining. The pleasure was almost more than she could bear.

Run, her mind said, even while her heart said *stay*.

Powerful currents raced between them. The tempo of their breathing changed.

Lord, don't let me fall in love with this man again.

But she knew it was useless to pray for the impossible. She had always been in love with Brick, from the beginning of time, through wars and holocausts and whirlwinds, from ancient Rome to the courts of French kings, from the savage frontier to the far eastern boundaries of the world. He was her heart and she was his. Wherever they were, whatever they did, they would recognize each other . . . and yearn.

Memories of their love filled her so that she could not move. The people standing around them ceased to exist. There was only the two of them and the explosions of love they detonated in each other.

From a far-off place she heard Marsha giving

commands, felt the movement of the Abominables as they were led away, heard the shuffle of feet as the stage cleared. Clifford's statement, "That's enough for today," seemed redundant.

But it was not enough. The soft touch of Brick's hand on her cheek, the solid feel of his chest against hers, the long, sweet tangle of legs . . . none of it would ever be enough. She longed for the miraculous joining of their spirits, for the feeling of soaring higher than eagles, wings touching, held aloft by a love so rare that only a fool would cast it away.

"They've gone," Brick said, his voice still soft with wonder and surprise.

"Yes."

"I guess we put on quite a show."

"Isn't that what we do, Brick? Put on shows."

"That's what we do, Helen."

They lay together still, his back flat against the floor and her body flattened on top of his. Both of them were reluctant to end the contact.

"I didn't mean to hurt you, Brick."

The double entendre was not lost on him. His face thunderous, he moved quickly, disentangling them and setting Helen on the bench. With one booted foot propped next to her thigh, he treated her to his famous "look," the lifted brow, the curled lip.

"It was just a spill on the floor."

"Still, I shouldn't have hit you so hard." She

pressed her hands together in her lap. "I'm sorry, Brick."

"Are you?" He captured her in his fierce black stare. "Are you?"

"Yes. I never meant to hurt you."

The morning she had left shimmered between them, a memory almost too painful to recall.

She had left him softly while he was still sleeping, sprawled in the warm bed where they had pledged their love in a hundred different ways. Blinded by tears, she'd placed the note on the nightstand where it would be the first thing he saw.

Watching him sleep, her heart broke.

Go quickly, while you can.

Taking the Abominables and the cat and only enough clothes for overnight, she had slipped through the house and silently out the door. The chill of spring seeped through her bones and invaded her heart. Standing in the dew, she thought she might never be warm again.

Spring would always remind her of leaving without saying good-bye.

Now, sitting in the empty building with Brick so close, she couldn't afford any weakness, couldn't afford to second-guess herself.

"Broken hearts are like broken bones; they have a way of mending," he said.

His boots thudded against the floor, and he strode off the stage, leaving her with her hands folded in her lap.

She squeezed her eyes shut against the hot tears. Raw and vulnerable and hurting, she sat on the hard bench and thought of the safety of her house in Georgia. It seemed another world away.

"I won't cry," she said, even as the tears rolled down her cheeks.

"I will be brave," she whispered, then she placed her hands over her face and wept.

FOUR

Brick stood outside the stage door sucking oxygen into his lungs like a suffocating man. Helen was inside, sitting on the bench with her hands clasped so tightly, the blue veins showed through her fair skin.

With every fiber in his being, he longed to go to her.

And then what? Wait around for her to walk out the door again?

He had been a fool to touch her, a fool to tempt fate. With a muttered curse he rammed his hands into his pockets.

It wouldn't happen again. He'd see to that.

Kicking gravel out of his path, he made his way to Farnsworth Manor and the relative sanity of a fiancée for hire and an evening of pretending that nothing out of the ordinary had happened between him and his ex-wife.

He was an actor, wasn't he? It was time for his greatest performance.

"Just what do you think you're doing?"

Marsha stood in the doorway of Helen's room surveying the disarray of clothing scattered across the carpet and over the furniture.

"I'm going back home to Georgia."

"Fine." Stiff-backed, Marsha marched into the middle of the mess and scooped up a handful of lingerie. "I'll help you pack."

Still clutching an armload of blouses, Helen sank onto the edge of the bed.

"Just like that? I'll help you pack?"

"Yes. It's cold up here. I hate it. I'll be glad to get back home."

They worked for a while in silence. Every now and then Helen cut her eyes toward Marsha, but her secretary's face revealed nothing.

Fine. They would leave. Just the way she'd planned.

Her heart was heavy as she put the last blouse into the suitcase and closed the lid.

"We'll leave first thing in the morning," Helen said.

"I'll tell everybody to be ready."

Helen glanced from the suitcase to the doorway. Beyond she could hear the dinner preparations of the Farnsworth household, the distant tinkle of silver against china, the muffled sound of footsteps, an occasional burst of laughter.

Brick would devote himself to Barb Gladly at the dinner table. And Helen wouldn't be there to suffer.

"You're not going to argue with me?" she asked.

"Why should I argue? You're the boss."

Helen walked to the window and stood looking out. Snow fell silently onto a land already covered with a fine white blanket.

"We could wait until it quits snowing," she said.

"Whatever you say."

"The weather forecast predicts snow for the next four days."

"I'll sit in front of the fire warming my toes instead of traipsing with you all the way across the estate to that drafty old barn Farnsworth calls a playhouse."

Helen wadded the curtain in one hand, released it, and wadded it over again.

"I don't suppose he'll say anything."

"Who?" Marsha pretended ignorance.

"Brick."

"Not likely."

"They can get someone to replace me."

"Certainly."

"I mean . . ." She wadded then smoothed the curtain. "It's not as if I'm the only actress who can play Katharina to Brick's Petruchio."

"I agree completely."

"You do?"

"Of course."

"Ginger Rutters will be happy to do it. She's always wanted to play this role opposite Brick."

"Lots of women would."

Helen whirled from the window.

"Are you saying Brick is appealing?"

"I didn't say it. You did."

"No, I didn't. I simply asked you the question."

Helen paced the floor, occasionally frowning at the suitcase as if it had done something to offend her. The afternoon in the theater filled her mind. Her skin still burned from Brick's touch.

"Well . . . he certainly has no appeal for me," she said.

Marsha gave her an arch look but wisely declined comment.

"Don't give me that look, Marsha."

"What look?"

"You know the one. The one that says I'm being irrational and overreacting." Suddenly all the fight left Helen. She sank onto the carpet and wrapped her arms around her knees. "Go ahead, Marsha. You might as well say it."

"Say what?"

"What you've been dying to say ever since we left the theater." Marsha pulled up a chair, folded her hands in her lap, and waited.

"All right. I admit it. Brick flustered me."

Helen pushed her heavy hair off her forehead. "It was more than that. Oh, God . . . Marsha . . . I felt the earth move." She dropped her head onto her knees. The tears that had not been far away since rehearsal started all over again.

Marsha dropped to the carpet, put her arms around Helen, and held on, silently lending both comfort and support. When the tears finally ran their course, Helen wiped her eyes with the back of her sleeve, then went into the bathroom to blow her nose.

With her tear-streaked face she looked nothing like the idol of stage and screen who had earned the adulation of fans around the world, but like a fragile, vulnerable woman, capable of intense emotions and great pain.

"There were no tissues in the bathroom. How can a man like Farnsworth not have tissues in his bathroom?"

She held a wadded piece of toilet paper in her hand, and behind her was a white trail leading from the doorway to the bed. She blew her nose once more, then began to unload the suitcase.

"We're not leaving," she said.

"I never thought for a minute we would."

"Why didn't you say something?"

"I figure when a person is upset about something, it's best to let him get it out of his system." Marsha picked up the toilet paper and threw it into the wastebasket. "Is it out of your system now?"

"Not quite. I think I have a few tears left."

"Then cry it out. My shoulder's broad."

Helen hugged her hard. "How can I ever thank you?"

"With a raise." Marsha never cracked a smile.

"If I paid you any more, you'd be making more than the governor of Georgia."

"I figure I'm worth more to you than the governor."

"Then earn your keep by making some excuse for me tonight at dinner. I don't want to be ailing. Think up something much more dramatic and important than that."

"You're plotting the takeover of a small island in the Caribbean?"

"Something like that . . . and, Marsha, smuggle some food up here."

"I hope my raise is enough to cover all this cloak-and-dagger stuff."

Helen made a face at her across the suitcase she was unpacking.

Marsha paused outside the door and shook her head.

"Lord, Lord. What's to become of those two?"

As she started down the hall, Barb Gladly emerged from Brick's room.

"That man is going to be the absolute death of me," Barb said.

Thinking of the look on Helen's face, Marsha hoped it wasn't death by loving, but she didn't say so.

"Great artists can be touchy," she said, inviting conversation.

"Grouchy is more like it. I went in there to ask him what I should wear to dinner, and he nearly bit my head off."

"Why?"

"Said he wasn't going to dinner. I told him Mr. Farnsworth would be expecting him, but he said he didn't care if the president of the United States was expecting him, he wasn't going."

Barb inspected her long red fingernails, buffed them across her thigh, then gave Marsha a sly look. "I don't suppose it had anything to do with what happened at the theater this afternoon?"

"Don't look at me. I never interfere with things that are none of my business."

"Well, I do."

Good, Marsha thought as Barb sashayed off. It was high time somebody interfered.

The peanut butter and crackers Marsha had brought upstairs after dinner would never sustain her through the night. Helen glanced at the clock on the bedside table. *Midnight.* And she hadn't slept a wink. She'd look like a raccoon at rehearsals. A *starving* raccoon.

She kicked at the twisted covers, punched her

pillow, and tried to forget that her stomach was growling.

"It's all your fault, Brick Sullivan." It would serve him right if she starved to death.

She looked at the clock once more. Two minutes after twelve. She wondered if she could possibly find the kitchen without being detected.

Throwing on her robe, she padded barefoot to the door, then peered up and down the hall like a teenager on an escape mission. Seeing it empty, she raced toward the staircase.

So far so good.

She kept in the shadows close to the wall. The third stair from the bottom squeaked, and Helen placed her hand over her heart as if she'd been caught stealing the crown jewels.

Laughter bubbled up, and she had to press a hand over her mouth. When she was certain that no one had heard, she made her way across the darkened hallway and toward what she hoped was the direction of the kitchen.

Her white silk robe and gown gleamed in the moonlight pouring through the French windows.

"Should have worn black," she muttered. "Like a cat burglar."

Laughter threatened to be her undoing once more, and she had to stop and pull herself together. At the rate she was going she could starve to death on the way to the kitchen.

When she had sobered up, she began her journey once more. She could see the kitchen door now, just a few steps away.

"Food. I hear it calling my name."

She put her hand on the door and pushed.

When the door creaked, Brick bolted from his chair. *Discovered.* Of all the rotten luck. And just when he was well into the cold chicken.

The door swung slowly inward. He grabbed the chicken and bolted for the nearest hiding place he could find. The pantry was crowded, but he squeezed in between the pickles and the olives and prepared to wait out the intruder.

Helen stood just inside the door, trying to adjust her eyes to the darkness. There were no windows in the kitchen to give even the faintest hint of light. Rather than fumble around in the darkness knocking over chairs and the Lord only knew what else, she decided to find the lights.

She ran her hands along the wall until she finally found the switch. Lights flooded the room, and for a moment she stood blinking in the brightness.

Feeling like a thief, she stole to the refrigerator and rummaged around until she found leftover chicken, green salad, and chocolate cake.

She tiptoed to the cabinets and tried not to rattle dishes. A silver fork slid from her hand and landed with a clatter on the floor.

Her heart pounding, she stood perfectly still

for the count of ten. When no one rushed into the kitchen to find her skulking around like a burglar, she carried her ill-gotten bounty to the table and sat down.

"Mind if I join you?"

Helen turned around so fast, she nearly toppled her chair. Brick stood in the doorway to the pantry, his hands full of chicken and his face full of wicked glee.

If she told him no, she'd be giving herself away.

"Certainly not." To show that she meant what she said, she shoved a chair out from the table with her bare foot.

Brick plopped his chicken on the table and caught her foot.

"Barefoot, Helen?"

"Yes."

"You always did like to pad around the house in your bare feet."

He traced her toes with the tip of his index finger. The heat from that simple contact left her absolutely breathless, but she wasn't about to let him know what he did to her.

"Some habits never die," she said.

"No. Some never die."

Still holding on to her foot, he caught her with a riveting gaze that sent a flush throughout her body. She sat perfectly still, praying that she'd have the strength to endure this late-night encounter with Brick Sullivan.

"I never could resist kissing that dominant toe." Leaning down, he pressed a light kiss on the toe he'd always called *dominant*, the one that extended slightly beyond her big toe.

The last time he'd kissed her dominant toe they'd been in the kitchen. Memories flooded through her mind . . . the smell of oranges and grapes, the taste of sweet juice running down his chest, the smooth, hard feel of the kitchen floor, the warm, wet feel of his mouth, the sensation of falling off the edge of the earth.

Heavy with memories, she sucked in a sharp breath.

Brick's black eyes held hers a moment longer, then abruptly he let go. Helen didn't know whether to feel relieved or deprived.

"There will be no replays, Helen," he said.

"Replays?"

"Replays of love."

"How do you know what I'm thinking?"

"Your eyes always give you away." He reached onto her plate and helped himself to a bite of her salad. "Love died the minute you walked out the door."

She started to jump out of her chair, but he caught her wrist and pulled her back down.

"Sit. You've deprived me of one meal tonight. I see no need to eat this one alone."

Sitting seemed easier than making another scene.

"You didn't come to dinner because of me?"

"Isn't the reason you didn't come because of me?" His thumb circled her wrist. "Well, Helen?"

"Yes. I was a coward." She jerked her wrist free, then picked up her fork. "It won't happen again."

"No. We're both civilized adults. Not only that, but we're professionals. It's time to act it."

"Why didn't you think of that sooner?"

"I apologize for my part in what happened at the theater this afternoon. It was a bit of childish revenge."

"Apology accepted."

"Tomorrow will be different."

"I agree one hundred percent. Tomorrow is another day."

"Yes ma'am, Miss Scarlett." Brick's grin was wide.

"Oh, hush."

Helen tried not to attach any significance to the easy repartee between them, but she couldn't help but compare Brick to other men. He was a giant among men, full of energy and fun and talent and passion.

She had fallen madly in love with him the first time they'd met. It had been at a New Year's Eve dance. She'd gone at the insistence of friends. . . .

"You have to meet him, Helen," they said. "He's gorgeous and talented and fun loving."

"He's an actor," she said, as if that alone disqualified him from consideration as a serious suitor.

"He's a great dancer too. Come on, Helen. One night of dancing. What do you have to lose?"

Her heart, for one thing. She was just recovering from having lost her heart to a man who saw fit to stomp on it and throw it away. Men always seemed to do that to her.

Betsy and Susan wouldn't take no for an answer, and in the end she'd gone.

The minute she spotted him waiting at the table with Betsy and Susan, she'd known she was in trouble. He had exactly the kind of looks she admired in a man, dark and exotic, poised and polished, self-confident and powerful. But it was his eyes that really got to her. Black as the pits of hell, they sparkled with intelligence and wit and passion.

"Oh, help," she said to herself. "I'm in trouble."

Her prediction was entirely right. One turn on the dance floor was enough. It was not merely the way he danced, nor the way he held her, both of which were wonderful. It was more, ever so much more.

Their hands touched. Her fingers wove through his. His thumb caressed her wrist. She drew slow, sensuous circles in his palm.

"You're a toucher," she whispered, leaning back to look up at him.

"Yes."

And they both knew. They were exactly right. Fate had brought them together. Every moment of every day of their lives had been leading up to the magical moment when they would finally find each other.

They slow danced . . . whether or not the music was slow. At midnight when they kissed, they both knew it was forever.

The next day headlines in the trade papers screamed "The King of Theater Meets his Queen."

She had found her king . . . found him and then lost him.

A great sadness welled up inside her, and she had to press her hands over her eyes to stop the tears.

"Headache, Helen?"

Brick leaned toward her, his black eyes searching hers.

"Can I get you something?"

The wonderful thing about Brick was that his concern was absolutely sincere. No matter what they had done to each other, he would never stop caring for her as another human being.

"No," she said. "I'm fine."

"Why don't I get a bottle of wine? Meals are always more civilized with wine, don't you think?"

"Yes."

She watched him prowl through the cabinets until he found wine and a corkscrew. He was giving her an opportunity to pull herself together. At that moment, she almost fell in love with him all over again.

She closed her eyes, letting the feelings wash over her. They felt so good, so very good.

Brick could hardly keep his eyes off her. Under the guise of getting the wine, he watched Helen. In her white silk gown and robe, she looked like a fragile, long-stemmed rose.

She was exquisitely beautiful. In the two years they had been apart he had not forgotten one single detail—the way her hair fell forward over her right eye, the blue vein that pulsed in the side of her throat when she was upset, the way she moistened her lower lip when she thought about making love, her walk, her voice, her throaty laughter, the soft, satiny feel of her skin, the tiny curve of her waist, the long, shapely legs.

His hands trembled on the wine bottle. Helen had no head for wine, and here he was in the kitchen pouring her a generous glass of chardonnay.

He was courting danger.

"Here you are." He set the glass in front of her, then watched her eyes sparkle when she glanced up at him. It was gone as quickly as it had come. Still, he'd seen the glow, felt the heat.

"Drink up," he said, straddling his chair.

"Thanks."

The blue vein pulsed in the side of her throat

when she lifted her glass. He had to ball his hands into fists to keep from reaching out and caressing the fragile, creamy skin.

"Aren't you drinking?" she asked.

"In a while."

Her eyes sought his over the top of her glass. *Why did she look at him with such intensity? What was she thinking?*

"So . . . tell me how you met Barb."

"Barb?"

"Barb Gladly . . . your fiancée."

"Oh, that Barb."

Helen narrowed her eyes at him. He reached for the bottle and filled her glass to the rim. Maybe if she had enough to drink, in the morning she wouldn't remember that he hadn't even known his fiancée's name.

"Where does any man meet the love of his life?" he asked, trying for nonchalance and missing. "At a dance."

"A dance?"

"New Year's Eve," he said, watching to see if his remark hit home.

Helen flinched. Brick was immediately contrite, but he didn't do a thing about it. He sat in his chair feeling a bit of self-righteous triumph at having caused her to remember *their* New Year's Eve dance.

"Friends introduced us," he said. "We knew right away that we were meant for each other."

Stony-faced, Helen slugged back her wine and

held out her glass for more. He filled it to the brim, then watched her take another long swig. Already her face was flushed and her hand unsteady.

He guessed he should be ashamed of himself, but he wasn't. A man who had suffered hell for two years deserved a little revenge.

Especially since he felt himself falling in love all over again with the woman who had betrayed him.

FIVE

Helen knew she had no business drinking so much wine. She'd never been able to hold more than half a glass without losing control.

Brick sat across the table from her looking dangerously delicious. Who needed control? What she needed was anesthesia.

She lifted the glass to her lips and took another swig. A drop of golden liquid sloshed over the edge of her glass and onto her chin.

"You should be careful there, Helen."

Brick's touch was exquisitely tender as he reached across the table and wiped her chin with his thumb—tender and addictive. She leaned toward him and closed her eyes. His thumb moved up the side of her face, drew slow circles on her chin.

Helen sighed.

Brick groaned.

His chair toppled as he scraped it back and stood up. Bereft, she looked up at him. His eyes were the color of the ocean right before a storm.

Helen knew she looked a mess, bright with wine and expectation. She drew her silky robe and the tatters of her dignity around her.

"I don't need your tender solicitations." To her horror, she slurred her words. Well, great. She'd just have to make the best of a bad situation.

"Those were not tender solicitations, my dear. I was merely wiping wine from your chin."

Brick never called her *my dear* unless he was furious with her. She could tell by his face that he was absolutely furious. And she knew why.

She had left him. It was the ultimate insult to a man. Not only that, but she had left him without telling him why.

As he stalked around the kitchen, slamming drawers open and shut, she thought about explaining everything to him. But it was far too late for explanations. It was too late for anything except trying to get through this charade with a little dignity.

"Stop slamming things," she said. "It makes my head hurt."

"Good." He slammed another drawer, then plopped back at the kitchen table with an enormous knife. The blade gleamed in the overhead light.

"What in the world are you doing?"

"I thought I would cut a little piece of that

cake you dragged out of the refrigerator." Holding the knife aloft, he watched her over the edge of the blade. "That is, unless you plan to eat it all yourself."

"Well . . ." Why did everything he say make her think he was saying something entirely different? She wet her lips with her tongue. "I like eating the whole thing."

"That's a dangerous thing to say to a starving man, Helen. Especially in the kitchen at this time of night."

The kitchen. Frought with memories. All of them delicious.

"Don't you threaten me, Brick Sullivan." Helen's legs were unsteady as she stood up.

"That's not a threat; it's a fact."

"Well, you should get your facts straight." She took the knife from his hand and leaned toward the cake. Her silk robe whispered against his thigh. His hand snaked around her wrist.

"What are the facts, Helen?"

Her skin burned where his fingers touched. She felt as if her entire body were about to go up in flames.

"The fact is, I'm the one who stole this cake. I deserve the biggest piece."

Their eyes locked, blazing. She was the first to look away.

"By all means, my dear." He towered beside her, then leaned so close, their bodies were fitted together like bookends. "Have the biggest piece."

She tried to twist free, but it was useless. She might match him line for line onstage or off, but she was no match for his strength.

The knife blade sank into the thick chocolate icing, then deeper, into the moist, tender layers of cake. A huge slice of the succulent dessert toppled sideways onto the platter.

They both watched it fall, their breaths sawing through their lungs. She made a move to break free. It only served to meld their bodies closer. She could feel the tension in him, the hard muscles in his legs pressed against hers, his heart thudding hard in his chest.

He held her wrist in a viselike grip. She could no more free herself than a bird could escape the jaws of a cat.

Helen swallowed her panic.

"I'm not sure I can eat that much."

"I'm sure you can, Helen. As a matter of fact, I'll help you."

Brick finally loosened his grip on her wrist, but before she could break free, his big hand closed around her waist.

"Brick. What are you doing?"

"Taking care of you. You always did have that fragile, helpless look that brought out the gentleman in me."

"Where is that gentleman now?"

"Right beside you."

"You're no gentleman: You're a beast."

His chuckle was wicked. Shivers skittered over her skin.

"You were always good at taming beasts, Helen." With one flick of his wrist he turned her so they were face to face, nose to nose, chest to breast, groin to thigh. "Tame me, Helen."

"Let me go."

"Afraid?"

"No. I'm not scared of the devil."

"You should be."

She might have been really alarmed if she hadn't been so hot and bothered . . . and so thoroughly anesthetized with wine.

In one swift motion he captured her lips. He was Sherman sweeping through Atlanta, Hannibal crossing the Alps, Tarzan swinging through the jungle with Jane, King Kong beating his chest in triumph.

And she was totally swept off her feet.

As soon as she could get her breath she was going to protest. Loudly. As soon as she found the energy she was going to clamp down on his lips with her teeth. Hard. As soon as the moon turned to green cheese she was going to stop kissing him back. Fast.

But for now, she was in meltdown. Her bones were liquid, her skin was on fire, her heart and soul and spirit were in flames. She wound her arms around his neck, leaned hard against his chest, and pressed her thighs between his. He was

all the things she remembered . . . and more.
Ever so much more.

He was gentle and fiery, poetic and passionate,
slave and master. What had started out to be a
punishment turned into exquisite torture. Pressed
together, fully clothed, they were making love as
only true lovers can.

"Tell me to stop," he whispered.

"No . . . don't . . . stop."

Familiar smells washed over her, the cool, out-
doorsy fragrance of his after-shave, the clean just-
pressed smell of his linen shirt, the tart/sweet
aroma of his skin, like apples dried in the sun. She
soaked up familiar tastes and textures, reveling in
them, drowning in them—the deep richness of his
tongue in her mouth, the feel of crisp hairs on the
back of his hands and arms, the wondrous feel of
linen caressing silk, the indescribable joy of hard
chest against tight, hard nipples.

He backed her against the table, lifted her up.
She wrapped her legs around him. Wanting him
and not caring if he knew it.

Desperate. Shameless.

He shoved the chocolate cake out of the way,
then spread her across the table. Silver clattered to
the floor. Glass clinked against glass.

Her robe fluttered open. Or did he pull it
open? It didn't matter. All that mattered was the
ecstasy of his wet, warm mouth on her breasts, the
exquisite torture of his hands molding her thighs,
parting them, delving inside.

Was it too late to stop?

"No," she whispered.

His eyes were dark pools with demon lights in the center.

"No, what? Stop?"

She drew a hitching breath. How could he stop a dying woman from reaching for paradise?

"I'm a dying woman," she whispered.

"Not yet."

He spread her out like a prisoner he meant to torture . . . or a banquet he meant to devour.

She was at his mercy.

Except that you can scream.

The voice of her conscience was far too small and came far too late. She was beyond listening, beyond caring.

He closed his mouth over her and devoured.

She had always been a noisy, grateful lover, and it was no different now. No matter that any one of a dozen staff members or half a dozen guests might hear her moans and rush through the kitchen door to save her.

She didn't want saving. She didn't want anything except the spiraling joy that carried her upward toward the stars.

Her fingernails dug into his back. She felt them score flesh, even through his shirt. Tomorrow he'd have scars.

She already had scars. Scars of the heart, scars of the spirit, scars of the soul.

He caught her face between his hands.

"You always did drive me wild."

"It's not intentional."

"Oh, no?"

"No . . . yes . . . I don't know."

His hot breath on her neck destroyed her reason. If she had ever had any where he was concerned. Marsha had said she hadn't.

She didn't know. All she knew was that she didn't want this forbidden ecstasy to stop.

He slid her straps down her shoulders, slid the gown down to her waist.

"My God . . ." Leaning back, he looked down at her, awe clearly written on his face.

Female pride made her want to gloat aloud. *Better than Miss Mt. Rushmore.*

Caution kept her silent. Tomorrow would be the time to gloat.

Or the time to regret.

Brick hardly knew what he was doing.

Revenge, his mind said. *Love*, his heart told him.

Reason had never been a part of his relationship with Helen, only gut instinct and raw emotion and the dead-level certainty that they had been brought together by the invisible hands of fate. Nothing could break that bond. Not their separation, nor their divorce, nor the two long years of silence.

She was good, so good. There had never been

another woman like her. He was lost in her sweet flesh, in the long, silky legs pressed around him and the soft sounds of satisfaction she made.

This is revenge, he kept telling himself. He would make her want him—already had, as a matter of fact. And when she reached a certain state of torture that only he could satisfy, *then* he would back away. Then he would leave her the way she had left him.

Ah, but not yet, not until he had feasted, had memorized, had absorbed the look and feel and taste of her into his very soul. It had been so long. Two years. Two lost years without the love of Helen, the love that had always been a miracle.

"Brick." Her whisper was anguished, desperate.

Good. That was what he wanted.

Wasn't it?

Her fingernails scored his flesh. He felt the sting through his shirt. His heart slammed so hard against his chest, he thought she must hear, must feel, must know. He skimmed the inside of her legs with his tongue and felt her shiver.

Power pulsed through him. And something else, something he didn't want to think about, didn't want to acknowledge.

Now. Walk away now.

Not yet.

In his emotional turmoil he must have made a sound, must have cried out.

"Brick? What's wrong?"

He raised himself on his elbows so he could see her. The strong kitchen light slanted across her face and her naked breasts. Any other woman might have suffered under the harsh illumination. But not Helen. She glowed.

No woman had a right to be so beautiful. No woman had a right to be so desirable.

Damn her soul to black everlasting hell.

"What's wrong, Helen? You want to know what's wrong?"

Her nostrils flared wide, and she reached to pull up her gown. He caught her wrists.

"No. Leave it. I want to look at you."

She didn't struggle, didn't make a sound. Instead she cut him to pieces with her eyes.

He felt lower than a toad, lower than a worm. That was all wrong. *She* was the one who was supposed to feel bad.

Silence thundered around them. The air became heated, heavy, electrified, much the way it does in prelude to a violent storm.

She must have made some small movement. Or perhaps it was he. A silver fork clattered to the floor. Neither of them moved.

"That body," he said. "That exquisite body."

Still, she said nothing.

"Damn you," he wanted to scream. But he was not the kind of man to curse a woman. Never had been. Never would be.

The silence was brutal.

Why didn't she say something? Why hadn't

she said something the day she walked out the door?

He raked her body again with a heated glance, then with the back of his hand, chin to navel, one long, smooth expanse of fragrant, silky flesh.

Once it had all been his.

"Perfect. You always knew how to keep yourself perfect, Helen."

"Does this conversation have a point?"

Her voice betrayed no emotion. But her *eyes.* They were kaleidoscopic, splintered with an unholy light.

"Yes. It has a point." He trapped her so swiftly, she had no time to react. Hands bracketed on either side of her head, he leaned so close, his chin brushed against hers.

"The point is this, Helen. Your body was *too* perfect, too perfect to be marred by children."

She sucked in a sharp breath. Still, she said nothing.

He pressed on, relentless in his accusations.

"Things were going fine for us until I mentioned having children. Then suddenly everything changed. I felt you pull away, Helen. Literally *felt* it."

Her nostrils flared again, and her lips trembled.

He hoped she didn't cry. He couldn't bear it if she cried.

Why didn't she say something?

"That was it, wasn't it, Helen? You couldn't

stand to mar your perfect body with a pregnancy. You didn't want my seed planted in you. You didn't want to grow fat and heavy with my child."

She damned him with her silence . . . and her eyes.

Say that's why you left me, he wanted to scream. *Say you didn't stop loving me.*

He was breathing so hard, his chest heaved. Sweat inched down the side of his face and dripped onto her cheek.

She didn't blink. Didn't move.

His body was so rigid, he felt tied in small knots. It would take hours of soaking under a hot shower to get out all the kinks.

"Are you finished now?" Her voice was polite. Remote. She might have been asking him if he'd finished his dinner.

Why didn't she react to him? That's what hurt him most of all, that she didn't react.

A line from *Tosca* came to him. "There is no greater suffering than the suffering that true love brings."

His suffering was almost unbearable, but he would never let her see. Call it male pride. Call it self-preservation. Call it anything. Just let him get out of the kitchen.

"I'm finished."

"Good. Then let go of me."

Unconsciously he had moved his hands to her shoulders. He was holding her so tightly, he'd made marks on her skin. Guilt flooded him. But he would make no apologies.

With elaborate politeness he pulled her gown back over her breasts, fastened her robe at the neck.

Shivers skittered through him. Best to ignore the feel of her skin. Best to ignore the heat.

She suffered his attentions in silence. He gave her one last hard look, hoping for a reaction, a sound, a tear. *Anything*.

Even her breathing didn't betray her. The front of her gown rose and fell as if she were resting in her warm bed instead of spread-eagle on the kitchen table under the glaring fluorescent lights.

Even now he wanted her. Even with anger scorching his skin and holding his muscles rigid.

He stepped back and held out his hand to help her off the table. She batted it back.

"Go," she said.

What else was there to do? He had hoped to humiliate her, hoped to punish her for leaving him. But the only one he'd punished had been himself.

He didn't dare risk another glance at her, didn't dare risk seeing how the silk gown molded her legs, how her dark lashes rested against her cheeks, how her lips had the pouty, slightly bruised look of a woman who has been thoroughly loved.

His footsteps sounded hollow on the kitchen

floor. There was no movement from the table. For all he knew, she might be planning to spend the rest of the night exactly where he'd left her, in exactly that position.

Every nerve ending was supercharged. Sight and hearing were heightened. He could hear his own blood roaring through his veins, like waterfalls when the snows have melted from the mountaintops and the rivers are swollen with too much rain.

Outside the kitchen door, he stopped. He was breathless, disoriented. There were no sounds from the kitchen, not even the whisper of her bare feet against the floor.

She might have been made of stone. Perhaps she was where he was concerned. Pure, cold marble. Untouchable. Unmovable.

Leaning against the door, he swallowed a lump in his throat.

His anger at her had already abated. He was mad at himself, mad at the way he had treated her in the kitchen, mad at the way he had let her get to him in the first place. But most of all, he was mad at himself for losing her. He should have been able to hold on.

What had he done wrong? Had he taken her for granted? Traveled too much? Spent too much time and energy on his career? Not satisfied her in some deep-seated way that was so obvious, he should have known without being told?

Pain. There was so much pain.

He stopped trying to analyze why he was hurting so. If he fell down the stairs and broke his neck, he wouldn't analyze the pain, he'd merely nurse his hurt.

He wished he'd brought a bottle of wine from the kitchen. It was too late now. He'd have to nurse his hurt the best way he could.

He pushed away from the kitchen door and started toward the stairs.

That's when he heard the crash. It was a loud muffled thump, like something soft squashing against the wall.

It was quickly followed by another noise. The tinkling of broken glass. Then the unmistakable sound of silver being flung about the kitchen.

Riveted, he listened. Was that rage he heard? Or pain?

"Noooo . . ."

Her cry of anguish made the hair at the back of his neck stand on end.

She wailed again, the long keening sound so tormented that only a rock would remain unmoved.

"Helen!"

The next cry chilled his blood.

My God. Was she killing herself?

"Hang on, Helen! I'm coming."

As he bolted toward the door he prayed that he would not be too late.

SIX

Chocolate icing dripped from the walls. Crystal lay in shards at her feet. Silver was scattered over the floor. The chicken looked as if it had been slaughtered on the spot.

Helen was only vaguely aware of the destruction. Pain blocked everything out, everything except what Brick had done to her, what he had said to her.

God, he had thought she didn't want children. He'd thought she was so proud of her body that she didn't want to mar it with a pregnancy.

Tears rolled down her cheeks, down the side of her neck, and wet the top of her gown. There were not enough tears in the world to supply her anguish.

She hated Brick. Hated herself. Hated the whole world.

A piece of glass crumpled under her foot. She felt a sting, saw blood. Her own.

"Don't move!"

Brick's voice was thunderous, his face mutinous. He filled the doorway, his heat sweeping through her as if somebody had lit a furnace underneath her skin.

She turned toward him like a sleepwalker, aware only of heat and blood and tears.

"Don't take a step, Helen." He moderated his tone as he made his way toward her.

Somehow the sound and sight of him had a calming effect. Logic kicked in. Rational thought returned. She glanced from his face toward the kitchen wall. Chocolate was everywhere. She'd made a royal mess.

"I didn't mean to," she whispered.

"I know. I know, love." Crooning to her as if she were a child, he picked her up and set her on the edge of the table.

She pulled her robe closed. "What are you doing?"

"Shhh. It's all right." He smoothed back her hair.

"No. It's not all right. Nothing will ever be all right again."

Fresh sobs shook her. Brick gathered her into his arms, and she leaned against his chest. How easy it was to cry on his broad shoulder, how natural. He held her lightly, rocked her gently as she cried for everything that had gone wrong in their marriage—the way she had bottled up her anxieties, the way they would leave to go their separate ways on the road when they both understood that the road was inexorably drawing them apart, the way they both covered their pain.

Acting. Always acting.

"Crying is good," he said.

Oh, God. It *did* feel good. Why had she bottled it up all those years?

She clung to him, drawing on his quiet strength. When her anguish finally subsided, she lifted her face and looked up to thank him.

His eyes and cheeks were wet with tears. Awed, she touched his cheek.

"You cried for me?"

"Yes."

No one had ever loved her enough to cry for her. The beauty of his tears so overwhelmed her that she was speechless. Only strong men allowed themselves to cry. Yet in their five-year marriage he had not.

They had shared their joy but not their pain. Why had they never shared their pain? Perhaps if they had, she would never have left. There would have been no need.

Tenderly she touched the tears on his cheeks.

"I wish . . ."

"Shhh." He put his finger over her lips. "Don't say anything tonight that you'll regret tomorrow."

He was right, of course. They couldn't go back. Especially not now, especially with Barb Gladly in the picture.

Her spunk returned. She knew the value of good exit lines. Leave 'em laughing.

"I regret this kitchen table," she said. "It's cold on my bottom."

"Sit there. You've cut yourself."

"There's glass on the floor."

"I know." He chuckled, sounding relieved, then lifted her foot to inspect it. "The cut's not deep."

"It hurts."

"I'll find something to put on it."

He left her on the kitchen table. Her bare foot swung back and forth, marking time, while he searched the kitchen cabinets and the pantry. In moments he was back, carrying iodine and Band-Aids.

His hands were tender. She shouldn't be letting him touch her.

"Is that better, love?"

She nodded. *Yes.*

His voice was sweet. She shouldn't be listening to him.

He held her foot awhile longer, watching her. His eyes were black, bottomless, fathomless.

"Sit right there," he said. "Don't move."

He went into the pantry once more and came out with a broom. She watched with fascination as Brick Sullivan, who had never known which end of the mop went on the floor, patiently swept up glass.

Every now and then he glanced at her and smiled.

"Everything okay?" he asked.

"Yes."

Why hadn't she seen that side of him when they were married? She'd known he was tender. It showed after performances when they would both come home tired and he would insist that she rest while he made drinks. But she'd never seen this solicitous, domestic side of him.

Would it have made a difference if she had? Would she have left him anyway?

"I probably woke up the entire household," she said.

"No. The kitchen's too far away from the bedrooms. Besides, these old houses are built like forts. We could have a war down here and nobody would know."

"We did, didn't we?" She grinned, feeling more like her old self.

"I suppose so. We always did strike sparks off each other."

"Yes."

She'd missed that, the way he could ignite her with a look, a touch.

He bent over and swept the shards into the dustpan. His body was beautiful, long and lean. The kitchen lights served as spotlights. Every gesture he made was controlled, dramatic. He was a natural actor. Even the simple act of sweeping up the kitchen floor became a production in his hands.

When he stood up, she clapped.

"Bravo."

He grinned at her. "What's that for."

"You make everything an adventure. Even sweeping up the trash."

"I thank you." He bowed from the waist, then dipped the mop in her direction. "My lovely assistant thanks you."

It felt good to laugh with Brick. She watched while he dumped the glass shards into the garbage can, then slid off the table.

"What are you doing?"

"I'm going to help clean up this mess. After all, I made it."

He picked her up and plopped her unceremoniously onto the table.

"There may still be glass on the floor. You could hurt yourself."

"It's my mess. *I'll* clean it up."

"I think I'm at least partially responsible."

She became lost in his eyes, in the deep, searching way he regarded her. Communication did not always require words. As actors they both knew that.

She opened herself to his unspoken thoughts. *I'm sorry*, he was saying silently. *I didn't mean to hurt you.*

"Brick . . ." She cupped his face, pulled it close. "Let's not hurt each other anymore."

"No. Let's not."

A muscle ticked in the side of her jaw, a sure sign of the strain she was under. She closed her eyes and took a long, shuddering breath.

How easy it would be to wrap herself around him and say, "Take me upstairs and don't ever let me go."

How easy . . . and how dangerous.

"Your hand feels good on my face, Helen."

His voice brought her out of her reverie. Too much was happening too soon.

She had to stop touching him, had to rein in the galloping stallion they'd mounted and were riding to the stars.

She folded her hands in her lap and steered the conversation out of dangerous waters.

"I'm not making any promises about tomorrow. Only tonight." She brought her breathing under control as he stepped back. "I won't hurt you anymore tonight, but tomorrow I quite possibly will go for the jugular."

"I wouldn't expect anything less of the great Helen Sullivan."

Did he use her full name to remind her that no matter where she was, no matter what she did, she would always have that part of him . . . his name? Probably. Brick Sullivan was bright enough to give every nuance meaning.

"Just sit right there, Helen. Let me go over this floor one more time in case there is more glass."

"I hope I didn't break anything that can't be replaced."

"You didn't. I already checked that out."

"Thanks."

She had forgotten that about Brick too. That he took care of her in small ways.

She missed that about him. Longing filled her, and she realized that she missed *everything* about him, the boyish way he looked when he smiled— *really* smiled—the way his hair swung over his forehead when he made love, the lights that danced in the depths of his dark eyes when he was happy, the deep, rich rumble of his voice, his touch, his laughter.

She realized that she'd fallen in love with her husband all over again. But it was too late, much too late.

Sighing, she slid off the table, picked up a cleaning rag, and attacked the chocolate on the walls.

Helen worked at the walls as industriously as she worked onstage, applying her full attention. Under the guise of helping her, Brick watched.

She was gloriously disheveled, totally desirable. And she'd lost control because of him.

An exultation all out of proportion to the deed filled him. Finally she'd shown him some genuine emotion.

What did it mean?

Nothing, he told himself.

They couldn't go back. It would be the same all over again. She'd cover whatever it was that had made her leave in the first place, and he'd pretend her leaving really hadn't mattered at all.

Maybe if the home were a stage, the two of them could make it as a team, but home was not a place to act; it was a place to be *real*. He wondered if either of them were capable of being real.

"Why did that cake have to be chocolate?" Grinning, she turned to him.

Irresistible.

"You have chocolate here." He rubbed a spot on her cheek.

She lifted her face. "Hmmm."

Dangerous.

He turned his attentions to the walls and applied what Fanny Mae at the orphanage used to call *elbow grease*.

"Use elbow grease," the cook used to say after he'd been sent to clean the kitchen as punishment for one of his many escapades. "It'll build muscles."

"What do I need muscles for? I got a brain."

"Wait till you're grown. Then you'll see what you need muscles for."

Dear old Fannie Mae had been right. By the time he was sixteen and out of the orphanage, he had muscles . . . and women falling at his feet wherever he went.

He followed a line of chocolate stain, excruciatingly aware that it put him closer to Helen.

He didn't want women swooning at his feet. Only Helen.

Her perfume was intoxicating. He took a deep breath, drinking her fragrance in. Long after she'd gone, the bedroom had smelled like her. He'd finally had to move into the guest room in order to get some sleep.

"Oops." Her hip bumped against him. "Sorry."

"It's all right."

It wasn't. The ease between them had lowered barriers he'd kept in place. If he didn't get out of the kitchen with her, he'd soon be out of control.

He put on some speed.

"I'm impressed," Helen said. "Have you ever thought of opening a cleaning service?"

"Only before every performance."

With Helen he didn't have to explain. The great thing about being married to another artist was that she perfectly understood stage fright, that quick burst of adrenaline that pumped through the system each time he stood in the wings, awaiting his cue.

"Me too." Helen leaned back to inspect the wall. "All done. Thanks, Brick."

She held out her hand. He started to take it, and then he knew her hand would not be enough, not tonight.

Without a word he swept her into his arms.

She stiffened momentarily, her eyes wide and luminous, then she settled back as if she belonged there.

She did. She would always belong there.

Heavy with the knowledge that he'd lost her, Brick switched off the kitchen light and carried her up the stairs. She rested her face in the curve of his shoulder. Her breath warmed his skin.

She felt so right, so natural.

He wished the stairs would go on forever. He wished the night would never end.

His footsteps made no sound in the plush carpet of the hallway. As he approached her bedroom door, his heartbeat accelerated. How many times had he carried Helen to bed? How many times had he spread her upon the covers and been welcomed into her soft, sweet arms? How many ways had he expressed his love for her? How many ways had she expressed hers for him?

The door creaked open. A shaft of moonlight illuminated the antique bed. Sheer curtains hung from the four-poster. A draft coming from the hall set the curtains swaying.

His throat was dry, his eyes moist. His heart hurt. His groin ached.

Helen.

Did he whisper her name or was it merely a cry of his heart?

She placed one hand on his cheek, softly, tenderly. He could see her heart pulsing through the blue veins in her slender neck.

One kiss, and then he would go. He pressed his lips against the blue vein, felt the beat of her heart, tasted the sweetness of her skin, smelled the scent of spring flowers.

Please tell me not to go.

Her arms tightened around him. Her eyes were luminous in the moonlight, luminous and filled with . . . What? Love?

God, let it be love.

God, it can't be love.

The mattress sank under their combined weight. Her hair spread across the pillow. Her face looked like a cameo.

Propped on his elbows he gazed down at her. Her fingertips burned his skin where they touched the sensitive area at the back of his neck.

Her robe had fallen open. He memorized the rounded curve of her breasts with his eyes, then his lips.

Helen lay perfectly still, her arms tightly laced around his neck.

Memories overwhelmed him . . . her long legs locked around him, her eyes wide with pleasure, her face glowing with fulfillment. The love and the laughter, so intermingled that it seemed impossible to have one without the other. Late-night forays into the kitchen, tasting more of each other than the fresh fruit they kept in a crystal bowl. Soft music playing and candles burning. Always candles and music.

His lips brushed against her skin. He felt the shivers that ran through her.

More. He wanted more.

He skimmed the neckline of her gown with his fingertips. The satin was cool to the touch, the skin underneath lush and warm.

She drew a sharp breath. Her back arched slightly off the mattress as she leaned toward his hands.

Helen. My love.

With one finger he drew a line from her throat, around the curve of her left breast, across her flat belly to the warm juncture of her thighs.

Her sigh was softer than a whisper, so soft, he barely heard it.

Joy surged through him. His touch made Helen sigh.

She arched toward him again. He traced her legs upward, from the curve of her foot to the inside of her knee. She bent her left leg, lifted her foot. The gown fell away.

In the moonlight she looked like a fallen flower, a creamy gardenia. He was filled with her, drunk with her. His senses reeled.

She spread her hands across his chest, fingers wide. Then in one slow, senuous move, she dipped a fingertip inside his shirt and drew erotic circles on his chest.

It was too much to bear. He would soon be totally out of control.

Tell me you want me, Helen. Tell me to stay.

He knew she would not ask, knew he could not stay. People who had been badly burned knew how to avoid the fire.

He drew a deep, steadying breath, then smoothed her gown down over her legs. Taking a light quilt from the end of the bed, he covered her.

Their eyes locked, held. Hers questioned. His begged.

The silence between them was deafening. His entire body pulsed with it.

There was only one thing to do. Leaning down, he kissed her cheek.

Tenderly.

She sighed, then closed her eyes.

He took one last glance, memorizing the way her lashes fanned across her porcelain cheeks, the way the moonlight illuminated the pulse that beat against her creamy skin like butterfly wings.

Go. While you still can.

He left her softly, his footfalls swallowed up by the deep carpet.

The door closed behind him with a finality that sounded like doom.

SEVEN

In the bedroom next to Helen's, Marsha lay under the covers wide awake and tense. She had heard Helen leave just as she had heard Brick's door open earlier.

She might be getting old, but she didn't miss a trick.

Her guess was that Helen was headed to the kitchen. For a woman as skinny as she was, she had the appetite of a stevedore.

Brick did, too, of course. But he was a man. Healthy men were supposed to eat heartily. And he was a handsome, healthy specimen of a man.

No wonder Helen had been fit to be tied after rehearsals.

Lord, would they get back together? Marsha half hoped they did, half prayed they didn't.

She knew Helen would never survive another parting. And until they straightened things out, a reunion would surely lead to disaster.

Her bedroom door creaked on its hinges and swung inward, leaving a small crack. That made twice since she'd been here, and she thought she'd shut it good before she went to bed. The way old houses shifted and settled, she was going to have to prop a chair against her door.

Marsha got up to shut her door and saw them —Brick and Helen. Together. Helen in his arms. His face tender, hers enraptured.

Marsha didn't mean to be spying, but she couldn't help herself. Lord, if ever two people belonged together, it was the two of them.

Brick carried his ex-wife into her bedroom and shut the door. Marsha dabbed a tear out of her eye and settled back into bed.

Was it wrong of her to hope?

Down the hall another door opened. Barb peered through the crack in the bedroom door, then scuttled back inside.

"Shoot," she said.

"What's wrong, honey?"

Matt Rider leaned against the headboard of his bed, the sheet drawn up around his waist.

"I can't leave yet. Brick and Helen are in the hallway."

"Brick and Helen?" Grinning, Matt wrapped the sheet around his waist and hurried to the door to peek over her shoulder. "Well, I'll be . . ."

"What does that mean?"

"It's about time."

He peered over her shoulder until Brick had disappeared into his ex-wife's bedroom, carrying his ex-wife with him.

"I guess this means I won't have to put my plan into action after all," Barb said.

"What plan is that, darlin'?"

"I was going to pick a public fight with Brick and return his engagement ring. Shoot, I was kinda looking forward to it."

Matt hooted with laughter. "You'd have done it, wouldn't you?"

"It was the only way I could think of to let Helen know I was out of the picture without betraying Brick."

Matt cupped her neck and threaded his fingers in her hair.

"Do you have to go yet?"

She melted against him. "I could stay. It's a few more hours till morning."

Matt took her hand and led her back to the bed.

From the moment Clifford had called act 2, scene 1 he'd been nervous as a bird in a pet shop full of cats. Much to his relief Brick and Helen Sullivan were breezing through the rehearsal without any signs of the personal upheaval that had marred yesterday's rehearsal—though they both looked a little peaked, as if they hadn't slept a wink. He guessed even actors were human.

In spite of their appearances, both Brick and Helen were in fine form. Brick strutted around like a turkey-cock, spouting Petruchio's lines as if he were the only actor alive who could do them justice.

Clifford thought that perhaps he was.

" 'We will have rings, and things, and fine array,' " he said.

Bravo, Clifford thought. This reunion of the great Sullivans was going to be a smashing success, and *he* was going to get his share of the credit.

" 'And, kiss me, Kate,' " Brick said. " 'We will be married o' Sunday.' "

Clifford leaned forward in his seat for the kiss. Onstage the Sullivans had always been magic together.

The moment Helen had been dreading finally came. She braced herself for the torrid kiss she knew was coming. She'd seen it in Brick's eyes. From the moment he'd walked onstage, his eyes had been burning with passion.

It was the very reason she had not gone down to breakfast, the reason she had been as late as possible at rehearsals . . . so she wouldn't have to have any personal contact with Brick, so all their interaction would take place onstage.

Brick's arm came around her waist. She stiffened, expecting to be yanked so close, she could feel each of his individual ribs.

"Loosen up, Helen," Brick said. "I don't bite."

"You'd better not. I have a lethal knee."

Brick turned to Clifford. "Sorry, Cliff. Let's take that from the top."

"Fine. From the top."

Helen mentally smoothed her ruffled emotions. Just that mere touch had been enough to set off fireworks underneath her skin. What was she to do? She had fallen in love with her husband again . . . and he belonged to another woman.

" 'We will have rings, and things . . .' " Brick's magnificent voice washed over her.

Helen barely heard a word he said. She was readying herself for the kiss.

His arm snaked out. She prepared to melt into him and instead found herself a good two inches away from his chest, not even touching.

His eyes were full of wicked glee as he leaned close.

Brick Sullivan was up to something.

Helen didn't dare close her eyes. Instead she kept them wide open.

His pucker was the most exaggerated thing she'd ever seen. He looked as if he were preparing to kiss a frog.

She braced herself . . . and felt a breeze stir

her cheek as he kissed the air half an inch from her lips.

She jerked back as if she'd been stung. Hands on hips, she faced the front row where Clifford sat with his jaw hanging open.

"That's the most cowardly kiss in the history of theater." Helen brushed her hair off her flushed face. "Even amateurs can do better than that."

"What's the matter, Helen?" Brick asked. "Feeling deprived?"

She wanted to claw the smirk off his face.

Deprived, indeed. She'd show him how she was feeling.

"You may be God's gift to women offstage, Brick Sullivan, but onstage with me you are nothing but a leading man. I expect you to act the part."

"And just how much acting would you have the leading man do?" His mouth turned up in devilish mirth.

"Enough so the audience thinks Petruchio at least *means* it when he kisses Kate."

"Ah, it's the kiss we're talking about."

"Well, what did you think? The weather?"

Clifford had resorted to groaning and was close to tearing out his hair. Offstage, Barb and Matt were laughing so hard, they had to hold their sides, and Marsha was trying to figure out what in the world was going on.

"Lordy, Lordy," she said. "Cozying up one

minute and fighting like cats and dogs the next. I'm going to quit this job before it kills me."

"Okay." Clifford left his front row seat and propped his elbow on the stage. "Let's do the kiss again."

Helen took her place. Brick winked at her.

So . . . he wanted to play games, did he? He'd better watch out, or she might give him a dose of his own medicine.

" 'Kiss me, Kate . . .' " Brick said, reaching for her.

Helen sidestepped. "I'd as soon kiss a frog."

"That's not in the script."

"What's the matter? You're an actor. Don't you know how to ad-lib?"

"Ad-lib Shakespeare?"

"Why not? Even Shakespeare could use a little improving after four hundred years."

Incoherent sounds came from the front row. Laughter from the wings.

"You're afraid of the kiss," Brick said.

"You're the one who's afraid."

"I'm afraid, am I?"

Brick stalked her. Her chin came up defiantly, and she stood her ground.

"Yes," she taunted.

" 'Kiss me, Kate . . .' "

"Never!"

His laughter boomed around the stage.

"A wicked wench does nothing but enhance a man's appetite."

He reached for her. She jumped away, laughing.

"Settle your appetite with a docile pussycat. I'll have none of you."

"You'll have all of me, or my name's not Petruchio."

Like a high-bred filly teasing her stallion, Helen danced around the stage, always just beyond Brick's reach.

Shaking his head, Clifford threw his script away.

"Is that Shakespeare?" Barb whispered to Matt.

"It's Helen and Brick . . . at their best."

Onstage Helen's Kate taunted Brick's Petruchio.

"What shall I call you then? A worm? A dog?"

"Best beware, my fiery Kate. Worms do turn, and even dogs will have their day."

"Not while I have breath."

"Then it's best to steal your breath away."

Brick lunged, trapping her against the garden wall. Helen felt the flimsy set piece give under her weight. It was either fall backward into an ignoble heap or lean toward Brick.

She took the lesser of two evils. His eyes lit with pure delight as she pressed close. She could have counted each individual hair shaft on his face if she had wanted to.

But she had other things on her mind . . . such as trying to breathe, trying to think, trying to tamp down the indescribable joy she felt at being in his arms once more.

" 'Kiss me, Kate, we will be married o' Sunday.' "

Brick's declaration of Petruchio's intentions sent shivers across her spine. He sounded as if he *meant* it.

His lips came down on hers, and all logical thought flew out of her mind. There was no stage kiss for them this time. Together they set off fireworks.

Clifford clutched the edge of his seat so hard, his knuckles turned white. The onlookers in the wings fell into awed silence.

The two onstage kissed as if they never meant to let go. Their exit was postponed indefinitely.

Helen wrapped her arms around his shoulders. He snagged her hips with one hand and her shoulders with the other. They swayed under the impact of the kiss.

His tongue found hers and locked with it in a delicious duel. She wound her right leg around him, and he broadened his stance to accommodate her weight.

"Break time, everybody," Clifford said.

But the two onstage didn't hear. Nor did they hear the exeunt of Marsha, Barb, Matt, all the animals, and all the stagehands.

Alone in the playhouse, they continued their single-minded exploration of each other.

Helen had lain awake all night waiting for this

moment, knowing it would come. She was powerless to stop it and reluctant to try.

Brick was magic. Always had been, always would be.

Was she foolish to steal this bit of magic in New Hampshire? Foolish to kiss her husband with such abandon, knowing he belonged to another?

Funny. She'd never stopped thinking of Brick Sullivan as her husband.

Her mouth, already bruised from his kisses in the kitchen, ached under his assault. It was a beautiful ache, a glorious pain.

What was she going to do when the play was over? How would she survive when the curtain went down and the lights went out?

Don't think. Just feel.

He pressed her against the wall, and it tilted dangerously under their weight. Steadying them, he propelled them to the center of the stage, still joined mouth to mouth and hip to hip.

Trapped by their passion, they stood in the spotlight so long that sweat began to inch down the sides of their faces. They couldn't get enough of each other. Brick pulled her close, molding her hips. She arched into him. He slid his hands under her skirt, shoved it aside, and fitted her closer.

Soon there would be no turning back. Both of them understood that, knew that there was only so much control that should be asked of any human being.

It was Helen who wrenched free. She ran a shaking hand across her lips as if she could wipe away all evidence of what she had done. But her lips kept the pouty, bruised look of a woman well kissed.

Brick shoved his hands into his pockets.

Did he do that to keep from touching her? She hoped so. She hoped she made him as crazy as he was making her.

"Is that what you wanted, Helen?"

Too late now for lies.

"Yes."

He stepped away from her so that no part of them was touching.

"So did I . . . God help me, so did I."

Real agony twisted his face. Shocked, Helen stood in the glare of the spotlight, silent.

He turned his back to her, rammed his hands deeper into his pockets. She thought he would leave. Brick Sullivan had never stood around to witness the aftermath of anything. They'd had fights in their five-year marriage. Didn't everybody? But the fights had never ended with any resolutions of the problems. Both of them were explosive. If one of them had the last word, the other always made the best exit.

The storm clouds never lasted long. He'd come smiling to her thirty minutes later with a handful of gifts, chocolate bars he'd bought at the corner store, a bouquet of wilted daisies he'd picked in the backyard, a perfectly shaped red leaf that had fallen from the maple tree beside the driveway.

She always forgave him. Who wouldn't? He had that special smile, that special touch.

Making up meant a torrid session in the bed or in front of the hearth or wherever they happened to be. They had camouflaged every problem with passion.

Now they were trapped on the stage, stripped of the one solution they'd always depended upon.

Helen's heart hurt so much that she pressed her hands over it to keep it from breaking and falling to the floor in a million pieces.

"I wanted your child," she said.

Brick stiffened as if he'd taken a hard punch in the stomach, then whirled toward her, his eyes blazing.

"Don't!"

"I want to tell you the truth."

"It's too late. The truth will change nothing."

"It will change this . . ." Helen spread her hands wide in a hopeless gesture. ". . . this horrible warfare that's going on between us."

"Warfare is preferable to hell."

Their eyes locked. For a small eternity they held the fierce stare. Helen was the first to turn away.

"All right, then." She wheeled around to leave. Her footsteps sounded hollow on the stage floor. She had almost gained the wings when his voice roared out.

"Wait!"

What was the point in staying? He was right. It was far too late to change things. She was making a life of her own, and he had Barb.

She kept walking.

"Helen." He caught her shoulders from behind, gently turned her around.

His face. She'd never seen a man's face so filled with emotion.

"What is the truth, Helen? Tell me. I want to hear it. I *need* to hear it."

"What good will it do? What has happened, happened. Nothing can change that."

"No, nothing can change that. But maybe the truth will take away some of the pain."

"I never meant to hurt you, Brick."

"I didn't know that then, Helen." His thumbs circled her shoulders. "Maybe I know it now, but I didn't then."

She absorbed the feel of his hands on her. No matter what happened between them, no matter where she was, no matter what she was doing, she would always remember the feel of Brick's hands on her skin, remember and cherish.

"I wanted your child more than anything in the world, Brick. I used to dream about having a daughter with your smile and your eyes. I'd dream about dressing her in frilly clothes and taking her to the park to watch the ducks on the pond."

Brick's eyes were moist. He cleared his throat.

"You don't put frilly clothes on kids when you take them to the park, Helen."

"Why not? I'd like to know."

"Because . . . you take kids to the park so they can get dirty."

"Why can't you get a frilly dress dirty?"

"You get frilly dresses dirty in Sunday school. When my daughter goes to the park, she goes in tomboy clothes so the other kids won't make fun of her."

"My daughter will *not* be a tomboy."

"She'll be a *Sullivan*."

Helen put her hands on her hips.

"And just what is that supposed to mean?"

"No self-respecting Sullivan is ever a sissy."

"She's a *girl*, for goodness sake!"

Suddenly Helen pressed her hands to her mouth, and he gave her a sheepish grin. Then they both burst into laughter.

"See?" she said. "We even fight over things that haven't happened yet."

"Yet?" His eyebrow quirked upward.

Helen felt the flush that crept over her face, heating her skin and making her feel light-headed.

"What I meant to say is . . . it's just as well I left. We fight all the time."

"Why did you leave, Helen?" She drew back into herself, but Brick would have none of it. He bracketed her face with his hands and tipped it up so he could look deep into her eyes. "You said you wanted to have my baby. Then why did you leave?"

"It's not important."

"I think it is . . . for both of us."

Helen tried to think of reasons to hide the truth from him and found there were none. He couldn't leave her because she'd already left him. She couldn't lose him because he was already lost.

The time had come to tell Brick the truth.

Brick waited for her reply. He didn't realize he was holding his breath until Helen began to speak.

"I didn't want to be abandoned."

"Abandoned?"

"Left alone to bring up a baby."

"I wouldn't have accepted as many road shows."

"I'm not talking about temporary abandonment. I'm talking about permanent."

"You thought I'd leave you and the baby?"

"Yes."

It was the most absurd thing Brick had ever heard. He was on the verge of telling her so until he saw her face, her eyes. Helen was dead serious. She had really thought he would leave her alone with his baby. He, who had grown up in an orphanage without another soul to call his own. He, who had wanted a family more than any man on earth. He, who would have fought anyone who dared suggest that he abandon his wife and child.

"But, why, Helen? Had I ever done anything to make you think I was that callous, that irresponsible?"

"It wasn't you; it was me . . . or rather what had happened to me."

Brick realized that he and Helen had never really had time to talk. Theirs had been love at first sight followed by a whirlwind courtship and a wedding that made the front pages of every paper in America. They hadn't even had time for a honeymoon, but had launched immediately into a joint project—*Much Ado About Nothing*.

All he really knew about his wife—his ex-wife, he had to keep reminding himself—was that she was a beautiful, talented woman who was his match onstage and off, that she hailed from the South, that she could throw together an elegant meal in fifteen minutes flat, that she loved animals but hated snakes and frogs, that she laughed at things he didn't find remotely funny, and never cried except at old movies.

Nor did she know anything about him. Maybe it was about time they got to know each other.

"I'd like to hear about your life before I met you, Helen."

"It's not pretty."

He waited, letting her take her time. Closing her eyes, she drew a deep breath. When she opened them he could see tears collected on her eyelashes.

"My father abandoned us when I was a baby. After three hard years, my mother married again. Six months later my stepfather left, saying he couldn't manage somebody else's child. My next stepfather lasted a year, the third only two weeks."

Brick could picture Helen as a small child, watching out the window as each of her stepfathers departed. How devastating it must have been for her. She must have thought *she* was the cause.

Suddenly his orphanage seemed a sane and safe place. At least he'd been surrounded by the same people during his childhood. Nothing had ever changed at St. Dominic's except the size of the chores. They had gotten increasingly bigger as he had gotten older.

"I'm sorry, Helen."

"I can't seem to hang on to people," she said.

"I was your *husband*. I had pledged to honor and cherish you all the days of my life."

"So did Roy Wayne . . . unofficially."

"Who is Roy Wayne?"

"The man I was dating before I met you."

"You loved him?"

"I thought I did."

"How could you *think* you were in love?"

For Brick, love had been so clear, so certain, as if the hand of God had written across the sky, *Brick loves Helen, forever and ever.*

"He was kind to me, affectionate."

"Passionate?"

"Affectionate."

"What kind of man wouldn't be passionate with you, Helen? He must have been a wimp."

"He was *not* a wimp. As a matter of fact, he was a weight lifter."

"You were in love with a brainless jock?"

"He was *not* brainless. And I never said I was in love with him."

"But you thought you were?"

"He seemed the steady kind."

"A *weight* lifter?"

"He only did that as a hobby. He was a CPA."

"Good Lord, a weight-lifting CPA? Why didn't he jog like sensible people? How much muscle does it take to push a pencil?"

"Why don't you ask him?"

Helen jerked away and stormed toward the wings. He caught up with her in two strides.

"I'm sorry, Helen. That was a silly argument."

She shook his hand off her arm. "All our arguments are silly, Brick. But that doesn't alter the fact that we argue about everything."

"Makes life interesting, doesn't it, Helen?"

"It makes me realize that my decision to leave you was the right one, no matter if my reasons were wrong."

Good. At last she had admitted she was wrong. Brick wanted to gloat a little, but he decided he'd best keep his glee to himself. After all, he still had a play to do with Helen.

He couldn't even effectively argue with her that her decision to leave him was *not* a good one. Even with her standing at his side and him wanting her more than he'd ever wanted another woman in his entire life, he was in no position to try and win her back.

He was a man tangled in a web of his own making.

Barb Gladly. His fiancée.

How was he ever going to explain her without looking like a liar. And if he admitted to being a liar about one thing, how would Helen trust anything he said?

Hoisted on his own petard . . . whatever the devil that was.

Helen waited for Brick to contradict her. Why didn't he? All he had to do was say the word and she would stay.

Helen, you're wrong, he could say. *You should never have gone.*

Or he might say, *Helen, I love you. I never stopped loving you.*

But he said none of those things.

Silence. It filled her until she wanted to scream.

Brick's eyes became shuttered, his face closed. What was he thinking?

Barb Gladly.

How could Helen have forgotten about Brick's fiancée? Mentally, she upbraided herself. In the heat of passion and the euphoria of finally getting an old burden off her chest, she'd almost made a fool of herself over her ex-husband.

She wouldn't be caught doing that again. A few more days of rehearsal, then the play, and Helen would be out of New Hampshire and out of Brick Sullivan's sight.

"I don't know about you," she said, "but I'm starving. I think I'll go up to the house and see if there's anything to eat."

She was almost out the stage door before Brick spoke.

"A little chocolate cake, maybe?"

Passion hit her full force. She squeezed her hands into fists and kept on walking.

That was another thing. From now on she wouldn't miss any meals.

She didn't dare get trapped in the kitchen with Brick again. The next time she might not be able to escape.

EIGHT

What next? Brick wondered. They couldn't go back and they couldn't seem to go forward.

He loved her. There was no question about that. He'd never stopped loving her. But even if he decided to try and win her back, where were the guarantees that she wouldn't run away again? Admitting why she had run was not the same as saying, *I would never make that mistake again.*

"Shoot!" He'd buttoned his shirt wrong. Helen was even interfering with his ability to dress. He rebuttoned it and left the room.

As he descended the staircase for lunch he saw Barb waiting for him at the foot of the stairs.

"Hi, Brick." She laced her arm through his, then leaned closer to whisper, "Everything all right?"

"Everything is just fabulous."

His smile was an even bigger lie.

Brick Sullivan. Actor.

❖————————❖

Helen forced herself to eat. One bite at a time. When the food wouldn't go down, she forced it with big drinks of water.

Across the table Brick seemed perfectly oblivious to her turmoil. His head was never far from Barb's; his smile was only for her.

Helen might never have confessed a single thing for all Brick cared.

Well, so be it. She had a life.

Didn't she?

The gym at Farnsworth Manor was fully equipped with the best machines money could buy. The exercise machines were in a carpeted area in the center of a track that was a tenth of a mile long. The weights were positioned along a wall of mirrors, and beyond them was a heated pool.

Helen stood on the diving board poised to jump. Matt Rider sat on the edge of the pool with his feet in the water. When Helen dived, he didn't even get wet.

He gave a satisfied nod. *He* could take credit for her form and style. He'd been her personal trainer for the last seven years. No other actress he knew had Helen's stamina. Certainly none of them had her body. She was in tip-top shape, each muscle beautifully sculpted, not one ounce of body fat, not one inch of sag.

"Water feels good, Matt." Helen bobbed beside him, treading water. "Why don't you come on in?"

"Nope. I'm saving my strength."

Helen didn't inquire why. He liked that about her. She was friendly without being nosy.

He was saving his strength for Barb. Now *there* was a woman. The experts would have said she had too much fat around her thighs and waist, but Matt was wild about every inch of her. (Love handles, she called her slight paunch.)

She'd get no argument from him. Content, he watched Helen make another lap of the pool.

"Five more minutes, Helen, then I'll do the massage."

"Fifteen, Matt."

"Ten at the most. I don't want you to overdo it."

"Okay."

She was pushing herself. It didn't take a genius to guess the cause.

The door at the end of the gym swung open, and the *cause* walked through. Brick Sullivan paused in the open doorway to assess the situation, then headed straight to the pool.

Helen was making her turn when he mounted the diving board.

"What are you doing here?" She caught the edge of the pool to anchor herself.

"I'm going to take a swim."

"The pool is occupied."

"It looks big enough for two."

"It's big enough for two, but I'm doing my laps."

"You do your laps and I'll do mine, Helen. And never the twain shall meet."

"You've got that right."

Matt watched the exchange with lively interest. After this morning's rehearsal, everybody at the theater had been making bets as to how soon the Sullivans would be back together again. He had bet by nightfall. The onstage kiss had made it seem like a sure thing.

And yet, they'd acted so cool to each other over lunch, you'd have thought they were sworn enemies. To make matters worse, Brick had been unusually attentive to Barb. It had taken all Matt's willpower to keep his silence.

Brick sliced into the water in a perfect dive. Matt had been his trainer, too, before the breakup.

He scooted back from the edge of the pool so he could have a panoramic view. He didn't want to miss a single thing between the warring Sullivans.

Brick cut through the water with the speed of a dolphin. Helen passed him going the other way. They barely looked at each other.

At opposite ends of the pool, they turned and headed toward each other. Matt noticed the space between them narrowing. When they met in the middle of the pool, Brick was close enough to brush against Helen.

"You're too close," she said.

"Sorry. It was an accident."

"Well, don't let it happen again."

Brick didn't look sorry at all. He looked pleased. Matt knew him well enough to know that Brick Sullivan never did things by *accident*. Every move he made was as carefully staged as one of his Shakespearean plays.

Instead of swimming all the way to the end of the pool, Brick turned and swam in Helen's direction. She was a strong swimmer. He didn't overtake her until they had reached the end of the pool.

She clung to the edge, treading water.

"What do you think you're doing?" she asked.

"Swimming."

"Couldn't you do it at the other end of the pool?"

"What's the matter, Helen?" Brick trapped her from behind, bracing his arms on either side of her. "Do I bother you?"

"What makes you say a silly thing like that?"

"Methinks the wench protests too much."

"This is not a Shakespearean play, Brick Sullivan. This happens to be my workout time, which you have managed to send into total disarray."

"There are other ways to work out, Helen."

"Why don't you try some of them, then?"

"You want to know one of my favorites?"

"No."

"My favorite workout is making love. Did I ever tell you making love for an hour is the equivalent of jogging five miles?"

Except for the color that crept into Helen's face, she showed no sign of being flustered. Matt had to admire her. She was as good an actress offstage as she was on.

And he knew full well she was acting. He'd been with her too long not to understand her moods.

"Why don't you tell that to someone who is interested, Brick? Your fiancée, for instance?"

Helen lifted herself out of the pool and reached for her towel.

"I'm ready for that massage now, Matt."

Matt stood up. As much as he hated to see what was happening between two people he really liked, he had no choice but to do Helen's bidding. After all, she was his sole employer now.

He looked in Brick's direction. "Take care of yourself," he said.

Brick merely nodded.

Just before Matt followed Helen through the broad double doors, he looked back at the pool. Brick was still in the deep end, treading water.

Brick decided he might have to tread water the rest of his life. He was certainly in over his head, and it was all his fault.

Helen had every right to be mad. He'd acted

like a fool at lunch, hanging on Barb's every word, hovering over her like a goose over a lost gosling.

What had possessed him?

A coward. That's what he was. He had taken the path of least resistance. Somehow it was easier to play out the game than to confront Helen with *his* truth.

He hefted himself out of the pool and shook the water out of his hair. He felt waterlogged. Burying his head in the towel, he massaged his hair. He hadn't wanted to swim in the first place. He'd just wanted to be near Helen.

The doors to the gymn opened once more, and Barb came through. In her hot-pink swimsuit and backless high heels, she looked like a pinup girl from one of those old World War II posters.

"Hiya, Brick. Where's Matt?"

"Matt?"

"Yeah, Matt."

"He's gone to give Helen a massage."

"Oh . . ."

Barb plopped herself by the side of the pool and wrapped her arms around her knees. She looked like a forlorn little girl whose lollipop had been stolen.

"The water's nice," he said. "Aren't you going in?"

"Nah. I don't think so." Barb inspected her long red fingernails, then looked up and contemplated the skylights for a while. "Do you know when he'll be coming back?"

"Who?"

"*Matt*. Jeez, Brick. Sometimes you can be so dense."

Brick came around the side of the pool and plopped down beside her.

"You got all dressed up in that outfit to come down here and see Matt?"

"Bingo. Give the man a cigar." Barb clapped her hands, then folded them once more around her knees. "We've been seeing each other on the sly."

Things were worse than Brick had thought. Not only had he put his own life in a tangle, but he'd also complicated the lives of two very fine people. He reached over and patted Barb's knee.

"I'm sorry, Barb. I've been so wrapped up in my own problems, I didn't take the time to notice anybody else."

"That's all right, Brick."

"No. It's not all right." He stood up. "It's time to straighten out this mess."

"What are you going to do?"

"Tell Helen the truth."

"About us?"

"Yes. Why should you and Matt have to sneak around pretending, just because I can't get my act together?"

"You'd do that for me?"

He leaned down and kissed her cheek.

"For me and you both, Barb."

❖————————————❖

Helen lay on her stomach with her face pressed into her crossed arms. Her head was wrapped turban style, and a long fluffy towel was drapped loosely over her body.

Matt stood with his back to the door, bent over Helen. Brick could hear the soft splat of his hands against her naked back.

It was time.

Taking a deep breath, he approached the table . . . softly so Helen wouldn't hear. He tapped Matt on the shoulder.

Matt whirled around, and Brick put one hand on his lips. With the other he handed Matt a note.

"Barb is waiting for you in the gym," it read. "I'll take over Helen's massage. Brick."

Grinning, Matt stepped aside, and Brick slipped into his place.

"Matt?" Helen's voice sounded tired.

"Hmmm?" Brick said.

"Use some more oil. My skin feels dry."

As Brick reached for the oil, Matt slipped through the door. Brick warmed the oil in his palms, then flattened them on Helen's back. She flexed her shoulders and made soft humming sounds of satisfaction.

In slow, sweeping movements, Brick worked the oil into her skin.

"Hmmm. Good," she said. "I like that touch."

All the things Brick had meant to say flew out

of his mind. He moved his hands along the length of her back. How long had it been since he'd touched her naked back? How long since he'd felt her smooth, silken skin ripple beneath his fingertips?

He caressed her once more, his hands molding the tiny, supple waist, the flared hips, then back up to her shoulders and down her arms. He was tempted to flatten his hands over hers, to lace their fingers together as they used to do when they were making love.

Not yet. He wasn't quite ready to reveal himself. Selfishly he wanted to continue caressing her naked skin.

"What's gotten into you, Matt?" She never lifted her head, but kept her face in her crossed arms. She sounded relaxed, almost sleepy.

"Hmmm?"

"Usually you're pummeling my back as if I were a punching bag."

"Relax." Brick had done enough voice imitations in his career to be able to sound somewhat like Matt.

"Not that I'm complaining." Helen arched her back and stretched like a kitten. "It feels wonderful . . . almost erotic." Her laughter was low and throaty. "Nothing personal, you understand."

"Nothing personal."

Ah, but it was. It was the most personal thing he'd felt in a long, long time. Caressing her was erotic, nostalgic.

He realized how very much he had missed Helen. Their love was magical, special. What had happened to take it all away? How had they lost it?

As he stood at the table massaging Helen, he realized how very fragile love was. They hadn't handled it with care. Sure, she had been the one to walk away, but part of the blame lay with him. Somehow he had failed her. Somehow he had not given her enough assurances that their love was permanent, that he wouldn't leave her at the first sign of trouble . . . or the second or the third. That, in fact, he would never leave her. He had been so absorbed in loving her that he had failed to *know* her, to understand her fears.

His hands slid down the center of her back. She made soft murmuring sounds of pleasure.

What if he failed her again?

The thought was sobering. If he stayed in this quiet room to tell Helen the truth of his deception, then he must be prepared to take the next step, and the next, to woo her and win . . . and risk losing her all over again.

Sweat popped out on his brow. There were no dress rehearsals for life, no repeat performances.

"Helen . . ."

She stiffened, then jerked her head around. Her skin flushed a deep rose.

"How dare you . . ."

"Helen, this is not what it looks like."

"Get out."

"I have to talk to you."

She sat up, pulling the towel around her. "Leave. Now." She started getting off the table.

"Helen, wait. Please."

She hesitated, slowly pulled the turban off her head, and shook out her hair. As she often did when she was upset, she massaged her temples with her fingertips, then ran her fingers through her hair. It tumbled about her shoulders in enchanting disarray.

Brick wanted to reach out, to touch her cheek, her hair. Instead, he waited. If he told the truth to an unwilling audience, all was lost.

Crossing her legs, she sighed. He knew he had won the first battle.

"All right," she said. "Say whatever it is that you came in here to say. But you must know this: I don't really care what you have to say, Brick. As far as I'm concerned, you're wasting your breath."

"That's a chance I have to take."

"Fine. Just so we understand each other."

She tipped her head to one side, waiting, and suddenly he realized that he had no idea where to start.

"This is not going to be as easy as I'd thought."

"Nothing ever is, is it?"

"No, Helen. Nothing is ever easy."

Restless, he prowled to the other side of the room, turning his back on Helen so he wouldn't be distracted by the sight of her wearing nothing but a towel. She waited quietly.

That had always been one of her good qualities, the ability to be still. She didn't have the nervous need of some women to fill every small silence with meaningless chatter.

Coward. Tell her.

He rammed his hands into his pockets and turned back to her. She hadn't moved.

"I have no fiancée, Helen."

"You've broken up with Barb?"

"No. There never was anything to break up."

"I'm leaving." Helen got to her feet. "I have no intention of sitting here in a towel, listening to your tales of romantic misfortune."

He couldn't have made a bigger mess if he'd tried.

"Helen . . ." He caught her shoulders. "Please don't go yet. I'm telling the truth badly."

"I hope you don't intend to keep me here by force." She looked pointedly at his hands on her shoulders.

"No." Releasing her, he stepped back. "You're free to go, Helen." She hesitated. "Leave." He nodded toward the door.

Still, she watched him.

"All right," she finally said. "I can't go. My curiosity would kill me." She gave him a rueful smile. "You know me too well."

"Or perhaps not well enough." He raked her

from head to toe with his eyes, loving the way she flushed.

"I'm going to put on my clothes. I feel at a clear disadvantage talking to you in a towel."

"Feel free."

"Turn your back."

"Turn my back?"

"Yes. Or close your eyes."

"You have to be joking. As many times as I've seen you dress . . ."

"You no longer have the right to watch me dress and undress. You forfeited those two years ago."

"I forfeited them?"

"Yes. That's what a divorce means. Forfeiture. No more rights. No more privileges."

"I never wanted a divorce."

"Well, I certainly d—" Uncertain, Helen paused. "Do as you please, then." She reached for her clothes.

Brick turned his back on her and stood facing the door, alternately whistling and grinning.

"Wipe that smile off your face," she said.

"How do you know I'm smiling?"

"Because I know you."

"All right." He made a dramatic gesture with his hand across his mouth. "It's gone. Satisfied?"

"Let me see."

"Does that mean I can turn around?"

"Yes."

Barefoot, with no makeup, wearing black designer jeans and a blue silk blouse, Helen looked sixteen. And extremely vulnerable.

Brick took both her hands.

"Helen, I hired Barb Gladly to pose as my fiancée for this trip to New Hampshire because I was scared to death of you."

"Afraid of me?"

"Of being near you, of working side by side on the stage, of seeing you across the table at every meal, of knowing you'd be down the hall from me curled in bed with your hair spread across the pillow and your left hand tucked under your cheek." He lifted her hands, turned them over, and kissed both palms.

"I had to protect myself," he added.

"You thought I would come after you?"

"No. I thought *I* would come after you."

Helen pulled her hands out of his and laced them behind her so he wouldn't see how they shook. Passion. Joy. Hope. All the feelings she'd kept at bay for two years sprang to life.

And yet, how could she dare to hope? Nothing had changed.

"That's totally absurd," she said, then stood very still, waiting for him to contradict her, *hoping* he would contradict her.

I never stopped loving you, he would say. *I would never abandon you. Certainly not with a child.*

He shifted his feet, turning slightly so that he was looking out the windows beyond her right shoulder. What was he seeing that held his undivided attention? And why didn't he contradict her?

"You're right," he said, still not looking at her. "The notion that I would come after you is utterly ridiculous."

A bone-deep ache started in Helen's chest and spread throughout her body until she felt heavy with pain, smothered with it. She had to get out of this room, out of Brick's sight.

She swallowed the lump in her throat and untwisted her hands. It was time for a great exit.

"Well, then . . . everything's settled." Her manner wouldn't have fooled a novice director. She tried for *brisk*, but what she got was *forlorn*.

Oh, help. Brick would surely see through her.

But he was still captivated by the sight beyond the window.

An exit was no good if nobody noticed. Where was a good exit line when she needed one?

"It's snowing," Brick said.

"I guess that's to be expected."

"Yes. New Hampshire in the winter."

The door was on the other side of a long, hot desert, and she didn't know how to make the trek. She glanced longingly at the door, then back at Brick.

His hair was longer than when they were married. She noticed how it grazed the top of his collar and curled under. He'd tucked his shirt in crooked, and it was damp across the chest and shoulders.

He'd dressed in a hurry. What had been his hurry?

"It's not as cold as I thought it would be," she said.

"Me either."

The absolute stillness in the room tore at her nerve endings. Her heart pounded so hard, she could almost hear it.

"Even Marsha is not complaining."

"She always hated cold weather."

They were talking about the weather as if it were of paramount importance in their lives. Helen had never felt so helpless . . . nor so uncertain.

He turned back to her so suddenly, she was caught off balance. *His eyes.* They looked shattered, too bright. Surely it was not tears.

She couldn't bear it if Brick cried, couldn't bear to think what it might mean. To him. To her. To them.

"Thanks for telling me the truth about Barb."

She held out her hand. He took it. Polite strangers.

"You're welcome, Helen."

He held on. Or was it her imagination? Wishful thinking?

Her palm still tingled as she started for the door. *Don't look back.*

The room was so still. Was Brick watching her leave? She thought not. Hoped not.

At the door she almost turned and went back. But what was there left to say?

She closed the door firmly behind her, then leaned her head against it. Her hand was still on the doorknob. All she had to do was turn it.

Brick was just beyond the door. She closed her eyes, picturing how he looked with his hair curling over his collar and his shirt tucked carelessly into his jeans.

She wanted to smooth back his hair, tuck his shirt in straight. She was losing it.

From inside the room came the sound of footsteps. Brick was coming.

Helen raced down the hall. It wouldn't do for her ex-husband to find her mooning outside the door.

Thank goodness there were no afternoon rehearsals. That meant she didn't have to see him until dinner.

No. She'd go out somewhere for dinner, take Marsha and Matt. It would do them all good to get out of Farnsworth Manor for a while.

She wouldn't think about Brick tonight; she'd sleep on the problem. And then, when morning came . . .

Oh help.

When morning came there would still be Brick.

NINE

There was no reason for him to still be standing at the window. It was dark outside. Nobody stood looking out windows into the darkness except a fool.

Or a coward.

Brick didn't like to think of himself as a coward, but that's exactly what he had been. He'd told the truth about Barb, but then he'd chickened out. In the face of Helen's resistance, he'd pretended that he never had any intention toward her except clearing the air.

Outside his window he could see nothing except the glare of snow—pure white shining through the darkness as far as the eye could see, each unique flake frozen and compressed with the other flakes until they all blended into one continuous blanket. Why didn't he have that ability to blend in? To be a part of the whole?

No. Not him. Not Brick Sullivan.

He had to be the strong, independent type. So strong, he couldn't even tell his ex-wife he still loved her.

He turned his back on the snow. Across the room his bed was the most lonesome place he could imagine being. So much room for one man. Too much.

His feet padded on the carpet, and his door creaked shut behind him.

Farnsworth Manor was a big place. There had to be a friendly couch by the fire somewhere.

Helen tossed and turned until she was so twisted in the covers, it was going to take a rescue squad to get her out. Sensing her discomfort, the Abominables took turns padding to the bed to nudge her with their big wet muzzles.

"Go to sleep, girls," she said. "It's all right."

But it wasn't all right. Even Gwenella knew it. The big cat prowled around the room, every now and then pouncing onto the bed and sniffing around as if she were trying to ferret out the trouble.

Helen kicked her covers back and padded in bare feet to the window. Snow everywhere. Shivering, she curled her toes into the rug. In Georgia it was perfectly all right not to wear shoes in the house during winter, but in New Hampshire it was foolish not to wear them. Already she could feel the cold creeping up through the soles of her feet.

Gwenella rubbed against her legs, purring. She leaned down to pet the cat and to retrieve her shoes.

Brick had been barefoot.

The image of him standing in his bare feet hit her with such impact that she sat on the floor. This afternoon she'd taken note of his damp shirt and the crooked way he'd tucked it into his jeans. But not the bare feet.

He'd been in such haste to get to her that he'd come without his shoes. In New Hampshire. In the dead of winter. With snow on the ground.

Never mind that he had been in the house. The drafty old house was cold. Period. Especially the floors.

The Abominables crowded next to her on the floor and put their big heads on her lap. Gwenella arched her back and huffed off, prefering to sit in regal splendor on the windowsill rather than share the limelight with mere dogs.

Helen hugged the Danes.

"He didn't even take the time to put on his shoes."

They licked her hands and the moisture on her face. Tears of wonder.

"Nobody has ever been that anxious to see me," she said. "And I turned my back on him."

The tears turned to remorse.

"What am I going to do?"

The Danes thumped their tails on the floor and lapped at her face with their long pink tongues.

"I have to go to him . . . but what will I say?"

The same restlessness she always got before a performance overtook her. It might be the performance of her life. She couldn't possibly do it without rehearsal.

Helen slipped her feet in high-heeled mules, grabbed her robe, and hurried from her bedroom, trailing ostrich plumes as she made her way down the darkened staircase. A shaft of moonlight slanted through the tall windows to light her way.

Here she was, skulking about the house at midnight once more. She covered her mouth with her hand to hold back the giggles. She felt as if she were in the middle of a made-for-television murder mystery, the kind that was always set in some creaky old mansion in an out-of-the-way place.

She could see the marquee *Murder in the Manor*, starring Brick and Helen Sullivan.

Brick and Helen Sullivan.

From the moment they'd met they had been a team. Her heart hurt thinking about their early days together—the late-night rehearsals, the greasy burgers eaten backstage at midnight, the flubbed lines, the laughter, the dreams.

She caught the banister at the bottom of the staircase and closed her eyes, remembering . . .

"We'll be America's sweethearts," she'd said, kick-

*ing off her shoes among the plastic flowers and prop-
ping her feet on a plastic rock, all part of the set for*
The Lion, The Witch And The Wardrobe.

*She was the White Witch and Brick was the Lion.
Always perfectionists, they'd stayed after the rest of the
cast and crew left to rehearse the White Witch's death
scene.*

*"The first couple of the theater." Brick discarded
his mane and grabbed a top hat out of the costume
closet. Setting it at a jaunty angle, he took a cane and
did a quick soft shoe around the stage.*

*"Care for this dance, sweetheart?" He swept off his
hat and gave her a deep bow.*

*She donned a red feather boa and a broad-
brimmed hat trimmed with ostrich plumes.*

"Enchanted, my love."

*Together they did a waltz around the stage, with
Brick humming "Shall We Dance?" from the* The
King *and* I.

*"They might call us the dynamic dancing duo," she
said.*

*"Sophisticated Sullivan and his scintillating
bride."*

"Who, moi?"

*She unslung her boa and tickled his face, then his
neck.*

*"Want to play rough, do you?" He caught the boa
and wrapped it around her, dragging her close.*

*"Yes," she said. He pulled her closer, and closer
still. "Yes . . . yes . . . yes," she murmured as he
lowered her to the stage. . . .*

———◆———————◆———

Heavy with memories, Helen made her way across the hallway and headed to the library. The cozy book-lined room was exactly the refuge she needed.

The doors creaked when she entered. She stood a moment to allow her eyes to adjust to the dark. The light switch was on the wall near the door, but she preferred the comfort of darkness.

The heavy draperies over the French doors leading to an enclosed courtyard were drawn shut. A small sliver of light made a path from the doorway to the bookshelves. Following the path, Helen made her way to the bar, her backless slippers making soft slapping sounds on the wooden floor.

Someone was tapping at his door. Brick opened first one eye, then the other. Where were the sheets? And what was that hard lump in the middle of his back?

The soft tapping sounded once more. Then he remembered. He didn't have covers, he was not in his bed, he was not even in his room. He was in the library on the couch. And a darned uncomfortable contraption it had turned out to be.

He rubbed his eyes and started to sit up.

"What will I possibly tell him?"

Helen's voice. Brick froze.

In the faint light coming from the narrow opening in the draperies he could see her long, lean body sheathed in a shimmery silk that reflected the moonlight.

Like a starving man suddenly confronted with a banquet, he feasted, letting his eyes roam up and down her delicious curves, curves he had memorized, curves he knew intimately. Careful not to make a sound, he leaned back against the sofa, trying to make himself completely invisible.

She held the heavy draperies back with one hand. Moonlight glimmered over her face, her hair. She had the pure untouched look of an angel.

"I should never have come to New Hampshire."

She sounded the way he felt—morose. And those were his sentiments, exactly. He should never have come to New Hampshire, for he'd known from the beginning where it would lead him.

To Helen.

They could not be in the same town, let alone the same room without coming together—magnets drawn irresistably toward each other, pressure fronts meeting over the ocean, comets colliding in the sky.

Adjusting his eyes to the darkness, he measured the length to the door. It was too far. He'd never make it without detection. There was nothing to do but wait Helen out.

In the long silence, Brick kept waiting for the crackle and hiss of logs in the fireplace, but it held a gas-burning fire. There would be no noise, only shadows on the wall and heat.

The sliver of moonlight faded as Helen released the drapery. As she walked across the room, firelight reflected off the sheen of her gown. Back and forth she paced.

From his lair of darkness, Brick watched. Should he say something? He was torn between revealing his presence and hiding it. He didn't want to scare her, but at the same time he didn't want to intrude on her solitude.

Finally she stopped pacing and stood with her back to him, facing the fireplace.

"I know this is going to sound funny," she said. One hand came up to brush her long hair back from her face. "Good grief. I sound like a simpleton."

She made a half-turn to the right and held out her right hand, palm up. "I should have said something this afternoon when you told me about Barb . . . Oh, help. That sounds so . . . uncertain."

Shivers ran down Brick's spine. Helen was rehearsing a speech to *him*. Wild elephants couldn't have dragged him from where he sat. He held his breath, afraid even that small sound would give him away.

"What in the world am I going to do?"

Helen walked to the window once more, pulled back the curtain, and stood looking out at the snow. He could hear her sigh, even from the sofa.

She stood there so long that he thought she might have changed her mind about rehearsing whatever it was that she planned to tell him. Finally she was on the move again, this time pacing between the bookshelves and the big square desk that sat in the corner of the room opposite the sofa.

Light from the fire caught the determined lift of her chin as she braced herself against the edge of the desk.

"I should never have come to New Hampshire," she said. "But now that I'm here I might as well tell you that I never stopped loving you, Brick, even when I saw you in the arms of Barb Gladly. I don't know what would have happened if you hadn't told me the truth about her. I don't know whether I would have tried to win you back or not."

Her delivery was strong and sure. She was every inch the actress. In her famous gesture of impatience, she shook back her hair.

"In spite of the fact that you told me you would never have come after me—"

"I lied."

Gasping, Helen pressed her hand over her heart.

"Brick. What are you doing?"

Brick rose from the sofa and stood towering in the darkness.

"I couldn't sleep. You were heavy on my mind."

"And you came down here and hid . . ."

"I wasn't hiding. I was sleeping . . . until you came into the room."

"Then you hid while I was carrying on like a demented woman."

"I heard everything you said, if that's what you want to know." His footsteps were slow and measured as he made his way across the room. "And I don't think you're demented at all, Helen. I think you are the most wonderful woman in the world."

Only a small distance separated them now. He stopped when he was close enough to reach out and touch, close enough to feel her body heat.

She stood tall and regal, her eyes riveted on his. Brick hadn't lived most his life in the theater not to understand when he was in the middle of a climactic moment.

Now was the time to speak the full truth. If he let this moment go by, there might never be another.

"Sooner or later I would have come after you, Helen. You are my heart, my soul, my life. Nothing can keep us apart, not time nor distance nor circumstances.

"I love you, Helen. I never stopped. Not for one moment, not even that horrible moment when I woke up and found you gone. I love you and want you as I've never wanted another woman. You never stopped being my wife, not in my mind."

"And you never stopped being my husband."

He didn't know who reached out first. It didn't matter. All that mattered was that they were in each other's arms, kissing as if they'd invented it, clinging so close together that it was impossible to tell where one of them left off and the other began.

He wove his hands in her hair and held her face in the glow of firelight.

"You are so beautiful," he said.

"You make me feel beautiful. No man can make me feel as beautiful as you."

"Have there been others, Helen?"

"No."

"I'm glad."

"I'm scared to ask . . ."

"No. There has been no one since you, Helen. You spoiled me for all other women."

"I'm glad."

"That makes two happy people." Full of joy, Brick held her close and danced her around the room. "Hear the music, Helen?"

"Yes." She cocked her head as if she could hear his imaginary music.

He grinned down at her. "Name that tune."

" 'Amazing Grace.' "

" 'Amazing Grace'?" He threw back his head and roared with laughter.

"Surely you haven't forgotten?"

"No, Helen. How could I ever forget?"

They had been in her apartment New Year's Day, only one day after they had met. The music had been playing when he'd walked in, a stack of CDs, mostly jazz and blues, dancing music, cuddling music. From the moment he'd started kissing her, both of them knew where it would lead. But they had held off, stretched themselves to the breaking point with anticipation, and when the moment finally came "Amazing Grace" was playing.

When they recognized the song, they'd both laughed.

"It *is* pretty amazing, isn't it?" she'd said.

And it had been . . . more than amazing. It had been a miracle, the coming together of two people who were destined from the beginning of time to belong to each other.

Standing in Farnsworth's library with the fire from the gas-burning logs warming their backs and the fire of love warming their hearts, he began to hum—"Amazing Grace."

Helen swayed against him slowly, seductively, her hips moving in hypnotic rhythm with his own.

"Remember the oranges?" she said.

"And the grapes?"

"You brought wine."

"And you already had a bottle chilling."

"Great minds . . ." she whispered.

"Great bodies."

His mouth slanted over hers, his tongue challenging hers to an erotic duel. She made soft humming sounds of satisfaction, the kind of pleasure sounds that drove him crazy with desire. He slid his mouth down the side of her throat, reeling from the taste of her, the feel of her, the fragrance of her.

He nudged aside her robe. It slid to the floor and lay at their feet. He lowered her onto that shimmering pool of silk, then knelt over her and spread her thick, shining hair around her face, just the way he loved, just the way he remembered.

She shrugged one shoulder, and her gown strap slid downward.

"I'm dying of passion," she said. "Rescue me."

"With pleasure."

To touch her with love was the most erotic thing he had ever experienced. He couldn't get enough of her, couldn't get close enough. He molded her with his hands, taking her gown on the downward journey, pausing to memorize her curves, her hollows, the exact texture of her skin.

She murmured his name, over and over, a litany of praise and joy and thanksgiving. He'd never felt such desire for a woman, such love. The need to possess her fully exploded through him, consuming him.

"I can't stand this any longer," he said. "Are you still on birth control?"

"No. After you . . . there was no need." She touched his face. "Brick?"

"You think I go prepared for this sort of thing?" He gave her a crooked grin.

"Oh, no . . ."

Her disappointment made him love her more . . . if that were possible. He held her close, soothed her with his hands, his mouth.

Relentless passion stalked them, passion that would not be denied. But he could not, *would* not risk getting her pregnant, especially since that had been the cause of their breakup.

Feeling his need to express his love through giving, he bent over her.

"This is for you, darling."

She spasmed the moment his mouth touched her. Joy rolled over Brick in waves, the joy of loving, the joy of giving, the joy of coming home.

She held on to his shoulders, her fingernails digging in. He'd have scratches. Love wounds. Badges of pride.

"Don't stop," she whispered. "You're magic. A miracle."

Firelight flickered across her skin, shone on the fine sheen of perspiration their lovemaking had raised. Wave after wave of passion shook her, and she cried out her joy.

He silently thanked God for old houses with thick walls, for big mansions with remote rooms.

Maybe the night would never end. Maybe the two of them could go on forever, tangled together on her silk robe in front of the fire, heedless of everything except their own private world, a world of wonder and joy, a world of miracles.

TEN

They crept up the stairs together at three A.M., holding on to each other and giggling.

"Shhh," she said, her finger over his mouth. "You'll wake Matt."

"Good. Maybe he'll have some condoms."

"You're incorrigible."

"You're wonderful."

She reached up for his kiss. They rocked together in the hallway, reluctant to let go.

"There might be an all-night drugstore," he said.

"It's snowing."

"Maybe Farnsworth has some snowshoes."

She wrapped her arms around his waist and held him tightly.

"Do you know how much I love you?" she asked.

"You'll have to tell me every day. I have a short memory."

"You? The man who can quote every line Shakespeare ever wrote?"

" 'How do I love thee? Let me count the ways.' "

"That's Elizabeth Barrett Browning . . . as if you didn't know."

He propped her hands on the wall above her head, trapping her.

"I know something else, Helen."

"What?"

"I can't bear to let you out of my sight."

Without a word she took his hand and led him toward her bedroom. Gwenella jumped off the bed and arched her back, then seeing who it was, rubbed herself against his legs, purring. The Abominables merely raised their sleepy heads and yawned.

"Some guard dogs you have there, Helen."

"Do I need to be guarded tonight, Brick?"

"No, my darling. You're perfectly safe with me."

"I don't want to be safe with you. I want to be wild and wicked and . . ."

"Careful," he added. "There will be no surprises for us, Helen. We've come too far to complicate things."

Helen smoothed back the covers, glancing at him over her shoulder.

"Are you sure you can do this?"

"One hundred percent positive . . . almost."

They climbed into bed, and he tucked her into the curve of his arm, spoon fashion.

"Hmmm," she said.

"My sentiments exactly."

Sighing, she snuggled closer.

"Better not do that, Helen."

"What?"

"Wiggle your bottom that way."

She chuckled softly, then lay very still. Their desire was a palpable thing. The air around the bed fairly crackled and sizzled.

"Is it all right if I move my foot?" she asked. "I'm getting a cramp."

"A foot is okay. As long as the leg stays still."

"The leg is attached."

"Try using the anklebone. It bends."

She jiggled her foot around. Even that slight movement made him groan.

"Something wrong?" she asked.

"Nothing a two-hour cold shower wouldn't cure."

"Sorry."

"Don't be. Don't ever be sorry for being the wonderful, desirable woman you are." Brick pulled her close and buried his face in her hair. "I love you, Helen Sullivan. And in case I forgot to ask, I want to marry you."

"Again?"

"This time forever."

ELEVEN

"This whole business is madness."

Matt Rider stood in the dressing room backstage feeling like a turkey getting trussed for somebody's Thanksgiving dinner.

"I look like a fool," he added. "Nobody but a wimp or a sissy would wear these things."

Barb giggled, then bent over to run her hands down his legs. Beneath the satin britches he was showing more leg than most because of his height.

"I kinda like 'em myself. Shows off your gams."

"That's not all they show off."

"That too." Grinning, Barb stood up to adjust his sword. "There now, you're absolutely perfect."

"This is a damned crazy idea, if you ask me."

"Brick and Helen *did* ask you, and you said it was a great idea."

"That's because I didn't want to hurt their feelings."

"You're a sweet man, Matt Rider." Standing on tiptoe, Barb kissed his cheek.

"Don't you go telling anybody. It would ruin my reputation."

"Seal my lips."

He meant to give her a light kiss but once he started, he couldn't stop. If somebody hadn't knocked on the door, he *knew* what would have happened next.

"Matt . . . Barb." It was Marsha, taking care of business, ever vigilant. "Are you ready?"

Matt leaned back and wiggled his eyebrows at Barb.

"If only she knew how ready I am," he said.

"Shhh. She'll hear you."

Marsha tapped on the door once more, sharper this time.

"Anybody in there?"

"Yep." Matt wiped lipstick off his chin. "We're here."

"Everybody onstage in five minutes," Marsha called.

"Gotcha." Barb fluffed out her skirts and twirled around for Matt. "How do I look?"

"Good enough to eat."

He took a step toward her, and she shook a finger at him.

"Naughty boy."

"Just going to take your arm."

"Shucks. What a disappointment." Barb laced her arm through his. "Do you think anybody will know what's going on?"

"Nah. This is the world's best kept secret."

Matt sneaked one last kiss before escorting *his* leading lady toward the stage.

Cramer Johnson considered himself damned lucky. He hadn't found out until the last minute, and he'd still managed to snare a good seat. Third row. Center section.

A stream of sweat trickled down the side of his face. He wished he could pull off his coat. Old Farnsworth must have ice in his blood. He kept the theater hot as Hades.

Cramer wiped sweat with his handkerchief and consulted his program. Intermission between acts 2 and 3. That was good. At least he could step outside and cool off. Maybe take a smoke.

He patted the bulge under his coat, grinning. Thank the Lord for blabbermouths. It sure made his job easier. Connections did too. If his aunt's cleaning lady hadn't been best friends with the upstairs maid at Farnsworth Manor, he wouldn't be sitting where he was. He'd be off somewhere drinking a beer and shooting pool.

He followed the action onstage. The Sullivans were good. Better than good. Superb. Cramer was no fan of Shakespeare, but he kept up. In his business, he had to. If he didn't, somebody else got the scoop.

Act 2 ended, and folks began to head for the lobby. He waited until the aisles were clear before making his exit.

It was hampered by two slow-moving little old ladies who had their heads together, more interested in talking to each other than in getting to the lobby for a breather. They were talking in whispers, probably thinking no one could hear, but to Cramer's trained ears it sounded as if they were talking just for his benefit.

"They say this is going to be the night, Maudie." The gray-haired lady who addressed Maudie looked as if she were too fragile to carry the many pounds of sequins on her dress.

"It has to be, Mildred. This is the last performance." The one called Maudie flashed so many diamonds on her fingers that she glittered more than the spotlights.

"How did you hear it?"

"The Bishop's wife heard it from her aunt whose best friend's next-door neighbor knows the upstairs maid."

"Then it must be true."

"Oh, absolutely. I'd put money on it."

"Pshaw, Maudie. You're too tight to put money on anything." Mildred clutched her sequined bag to her sequined breast. "Oh, I do hope it's true. Just think. We'll be *witnesses.*"

Cramer was sweating in earnest by the time he

reached the lobby. If those two old ladies knew, how many other people did?

He hurried through the glass double doors into the New Hampshire night. A full moon sparkled on the snow. Winter wonderland.

But not if he didn't get an exclusive. He barely took the time to draw a deep breath before hurrying back inside and hustling down the aisle to his seat. Couldn't take the chance of getting stranded while somebody else got the story.

The curtain came up and act 3 proceeded on schedule.

" 'I must, forsooth, be forc'd to give my hand, oppos'd against my heart, unto a mad-brain rudesby, full of spleen; who woo'd in haste, and means to wed at leisure.' "

Helen Sullivan had never looked more radiant as she delivered Katharine's prewedding speech.

Cramer felt all his muscles tense.

" 'I told you, I, he was a frantic fool, hiding his bitter jests in blunt behaviour. And, to be noted for a merry man, he'll woo a thousand, 'point the day of marriage, make friends, invite them, and proclaim the banns; yet never means to wed where he hath woo'd.' "

There was a stir in the audience as Brick Sullivan entered from the wings riding on the most broken-down, swaybacked horse Cramer had ever seen. They must have taken the nag directly from the glue factory.

The horse was exactly as Shakespeare had described it, as were the clothes Brick Sullivan wore —an old jerkin that looked as if the mice had chewed it, britches with holes in them, mismatched boots, one laced and one buckled, and an old rusty sword with a broken hilt.

"Woo'd you I did, and wed you I will." Brick's Petruchio dismounted his nag and swooped upon Helen like a falcon diving for his prey. He circled her waist and swept her into his arms. "Kiss me Kate, for I desire a taste of honey before I wed."

The lines he had quoted were not Shakespeare, and the kiss he gave his ex-wife was *definitely* not a stage kiss. Cramer stuck his hand underneath his coat to feel his camera.

The kiss lasted so long that a murmur of appreciation went up from the audience.

Brick Sullivan finally released Helen and dazzled the audience with his famous grin.

"Come, come, sweet Kate," he roared, "you call that a kiss. 'Tis but a slight sting of the bee."

"Touch me again, and I'll show you my stinger."

"Your stinger I'll take, but later, sweet Kate. Unless you desire an audience when you give me all?"

"I'll give you nothing."

"I take what I want, not ask. And sweet Kate, I'm taking *you*."

Brick swept her into his arms once more, then leaned her over backward until her hair was almost sweeping the floor.

The audience sighed their approval. Cramer listened for whispered comments about how the play had drastically departed from the original, but there were none. No actors alive could get by with rewriting Shakespeare except the Sullivans.

He pulled his notepad out and began to scribble.

" 'Of all mad matches, never was the like!' " One of the characters onstage spoke the line that sounded like the *real* Shakespeare, but Cramer was beyond caring. From offstage came the sound of minstrel music. It grew louder and louder, until finally the minstrels paraded onto the stage, followed by a man in priest's garb.

"I'll be a son of a gun." Cramer jerked out his camera. The priest was no actor; he was Father Glenn O'Malley from the St. James Catholic Church in nearby Concord.

"Come, come," Brick said. "Don't dawdle, parson, for I would wed the wench."

"No wench am I, and no wife I'll be."

Brick chucked Helen under the chin, then kissed her thoroughly once more, much to the delight of the audience.

"Some call you an irksome, brawling scold, a waspish, ill-tempered wildcat." Brick ran his hands the length of Helen's back, letting them come to rest on her derriere. "But I call you sweeter than a honeycomb, and your nectar I'll suck before the day's end."

"Twill end before you wish if you don't put your hands in a proper place."

"Nay, sweet Kate. All is proper for all will be mine." Brick clapped the priest on the shoulder. "On with the wedding."

Brick took Helen's hand, and the two of them stood before the priest.

Others in the audience recognized the priest.

"That's Father O'Malley," one said.

"The wedding's real."

"Brick Sullivan's going to remarry his wife."

Indeed, he was . . . and Cramer was going to have the exclusive. Chortling with glee, he stood up to record the event for the first page of the morning edition . . . and found himself in the company of eight other newspapermen, popping up all over the theater like toast.

"So much for an exclusive," he muttered.

Onstage Brick was only vaguely aware of the glare of flashbulbs. He had eyes only for Helen. She looked beautiful and very, very vulnerable. Her hand trembled in his as she said her vows.

Once again they had rushed to the altar without spending much time in courtship. But they were older now, and wiser. The second time around would be the charm.

Wouldn't it?

TWELVE

Headlines around the nation carried the news of their wedding. "Reunion of the Famous Sullivans Permanent." "Petruchio Weds Kate; Brick Weds Helen." "The Sullivans Exchange Vows On-stage." "Love Thaws in the Frozen North." "Shakespeare Rewritten by the Famous Sullivans."

The newspapers were scattered around their honeymoon suite. After the play closed, they'd graciously granted interviews, then ducked out to hop a private plane to New York.

They hadn't even had a honeymoon the first time. They'd both vowed to do everything right this time.

Brick came through the door softly, determined to surprise his wife, then stood in the bedroom in rapt silence, watching her. She was even more beautiful asleep than awake, if that were possible. The bloom of their recent lovemaking still colored her skin, and the peace of repose eased her entire body in total relaxation.

One arm was curled under her pillow, the other hanging over the bed. One leg was tucked securely under the sheets, the other boldly sprawled in a position both provocative and vulnerable. She still wore high heels and pearls.

To think that he'd once lost her. He batted the wetness from the corner of his eyes.

Never again. He would do everything in his power to keep her this time.

He approached the bed softly. She stirred, sighing, then settled back with a smile on her face. He placed a single long-stemmed red rose on her pillow.

One of her eyelids fluttered open. Then the other.

"Good afternoon, sleepyhead." He bent to kiss her lips.

"My, how time flies when you're having fun." She gave him a dazzling smile.

"Did you have fun?"

"Fishing?"

"Yes. You know how actors are, always looking for rave reviews."

"Superb. Stupendous. Incredible. Awesome. Miraculous . . . More."

Laughing, he sat down beside her. The mattress sagged under his weight, and the rose rolled off the pillow. He picked it up and caressed her cheeks with the petals.

"I like those reviews. Especially the last one." He moved the petals over her lips. They parted, and her tongue darted out to taste the rose.

"Hmmm. Good. More."

He trailed the rose down the side of her throat, then pushed aside the sheet to tease her nipples.

"Does this rose have thorns?" she asked.

"I plucked them all off." The rose slowly circled her breasts. She arched into its velvety caress. "I've banished thorns from your life forever."

"My hero."

He leaned down and followed the path of the rose with his tongue. Shivers ran through her. Brick loved the way she responded to his foreplay, loved watching her reactions.

"You are the most incredible woman in the world. Did I ever tell you that?" He slid the rose over her flat abdomen, pausing at the indention of her navel to twirl the petals in a circular motion. Her shiver was his reward.

"About six times last night and in the wee hours of the morning."

Her hand moved to lower the sheet, but he covered it with his. One of the best parts of loving was the anticipation.

"Seven."

He drew the rose back over her nipples, slowly caressing. Her hand trembled on the sheet.

"You counted?"

"A guy has to keep track of his performances."

He wet the rose with his tongue, then teased her lips with the damp petals. A pink glow flushed her cheeks.

"Don't expect me to help you keep track. I'm too busy with other things."

The damp rose trailed downward once more, and her body grew taut as a bowstring. Such a small thing. A damp rose. And yet it ignited their passion as quickly as the most erotic, soul-searing kisses.

He leaned back and carefully folded the sheet down, revealing Helen inch by incredible inch. The pearls gleamed against her skin; the black backless high heels shaped her already perfect calves, and the black lace G-string enhanced rather than covered.

"A lady should always wear pearls with basic black," she'd said, posing the night before in the bathroom doorway.

"Just don't expect me to wear a tux," he'd replied. "It might hamper things a bit."

Remembering, he covered the tiny G-string with one hand, letting it rest lightly, fingers barely brushing her exposed skin. Her eyes widened, and her breath hitched in her throat.

"That's how I want you to be," he said, pressing closer to her, close enough to feel her heat. "Busy with other things." His hand eased aside the bit of lace, his fingers found the heat. "Namely me."

She sucked in a sharp breath. She was already swollen from their night of loving, and he brought her quickly to the edge.

"Brick . . ." His name ended on a rising crescendo.

Her cries of pleasure ignited him to the boiling point. And still he held back. While the last notes of release still quivered in her throat, he bent over her, reveling in the sweet, hot feel of her intimate flesh against his lips, and brought her quickly back to climax.

"Brick . . . please."

Drugged with her sweetness, he propped his arms on either side of her head and leaned so close, he almost drowned in her eyes.

"Do you love me, Helen?"

"Yes."

"Say it. Say the words."

"I love you, Brick Sullivan. I adore you."

"Tell me how much."

"More than life itself."

He tried to let the present joy tamp down the fear in him, the fear that was always in him. Helen had said the words to him, freely and often during their five-year marriage. "I love you, Brick. I adore you. More than life itself." And yet words hadn't kept her from running away.

Would she run again?

The terror threatened to take over, to rob him of the present.

Her arms stole around his neck, and she pulled him down so she could press kisses all over his cheeks, his neck, his shoulders, then back to his lips.

"You know I love you, Brick. I always have and always will. This time forever."

Had she said *forever* the first time around? Brick couldn't remember.

"I want you inside me," she whispered. "Fill me, Brick."

He could lose his fear in her and find a wonder that would ease his mind and heart and soul. And yet, he knew that when the lovemaking was over, the gnawing fear would return. Had he been careful enough? Had the birth control method worked? What if she got pregnant?

He felt a tremor run up his arms and through his body. His pulse pounded so hard, he could almost hear it. His need to fill her was so great, it was almost physical pain.

"Now," she whispered. Her hot, wet kisses inflamed him; her tongue drove him over the edge.

He covered her, merged with her, melted in her. Sweet gentleness and slow tenderness were rarely a part of their lovemaking, had never been a part of it. Their volatile personalities required the same volatility of their bodies.

She wrapped her legs around his waist, shudders already rippling through her. Her cries of pleasure rose and fell like music on his ears. When they'd first made love so many years ago, he'd thought they were cries of distress. Alarmed, he'd pulled back.

"Am I hurting you?" he'd asked.

"No. Oh, no. Please don't stop. Don't go away."

Now, he looked down into her face, loving to see the play of intense emotions. She was totally lost in him, as he was in her. Over and over he watched her shatter, watched the dark fires of passion take over until there was nothing but the wonder and the terror of completely belonging to another, of merging until self was lost and they were one.

Sweat slicked his body. She wrapped her legs higher, around his neck. The heels of her shoes nicked his skin. Her fingernails were sunk deep into his flesh.

Wondrous possession. Terrifying joy.

They moved together as one, as if they belonged, as if they had always belonged. Never stopping, he looked down at her.

"This is a game, Helen, and there's only one rule."

"What is it?"

"You have to keep your eyes open."

"I thought I did."

"No."

"I'm making no rash promises, but I'll try."

The dark fires of love shone in her eyes. Sun

slanting through the windows enhanced the glow. Brick felt as if he'd been crowned king of the world.

Helen. His love, his life, his joy.

His passion built until all logical thought left his mind. Ancient rhythms overtook them, and they danced to the music that had moved them through the centuries, the songs that had triggered erotic impulses in their past lives, in green meadows beside quiet streams where the lamb and the lion lay side by side, on rolling hills high above cities that lay under siege, in deep caverns removed from civilizations that were falling. Over mountains and through storms and across seas they had pledged their love again and again. A love that would never die.

Buried deep, he lost himself, his cry of completion blending with hers.

He felt her arms steal around him, felt her hands glide gently over his sweat-slicked back. He rested his forehead in the crook of her shoulder, and she rocked him, crooning love songs that had no words, only meanings, only wonderful, joyous meanings.

For a while yet, time would cease to exist. Brick closed his eyes, willing it always to be that way, willing the world to stay back, willing reality to leave them alone.

Distant sounds of the city drifted up to them —street vendors hawking their wares, the blare of horns from impatient taxi drivers, the squeal of tires, the rumble of trains, and the roar of jets.

"I scratched you," Helen said, her hands roaming down his back. "I'm sorry."

As beautiful as her voice was, Brick didn't want to hear it. Not yet. He wasn't ready to enter the world where people often conversed without communicating.

"It's nothing," he said.

"I'll put something on it."

To satisfy her, he lay still while she went into the bathroom and came back with first-aid cream. When she smeared it on, he didn't tell her that she should wash the wound first, didn't care that she was a lousy nurse. Flushed and lovely, she bent over him, her hair touching his shoulder.

He ran his hands down the length of her legs.

"Hmmm," she said, stretching like a kitten. "Nice."

"Why don't I rub something on you?"

"First-aid cream?"

He laughed. She smiled.

"Guess again."

He reached for her, but she sidestepped.

"Not yet," she said.

He folded one arm under his head and watched as she crossed the room in her highheels and pearls. He would never tire of watching her.

"Close your eyes," she said.

"And miss all the fun?"

"It's a surprise."

Grinning, he closed his eyes. He didn't have to see to know when she stood beside him. He could smell her French perfume, tea rose from the Parfumeur, Ltd. in New Orleans.

"Keep them closed," she whispered, leaning over him so that her hair brushed against his chest. She caught one of his wrists and wrapped something silky and cool around it.

A satin ribbon. She'd tied him to the bed once in New Orleans.

"I already love this surprise," he said.

"Stretch out a little, sweet one."

"Like this?" He spread-eagled on the bed.

There was no reply, nothing except the sound of breathing.

"You're gorgeous, Brick. Did I ever tell you that?"

"Once or twice." She'd always been more than generous with compliments. She'd always made him feel like a hero.

She touched his chest, tangled her hands in his chest hair.

"Beautiful," she whispered.

"It's all yours."

Laughing, she bound him to the bed with scarlet ribbons.

"Now you are my slave," she said.

He didn't bother to tell her that he'd always been her slave. He was too busy with other things.

THIRTEEN

As Brick sauntered up the brick walkway to his home, he noticed a spot of yellow under the big oak tree in their front yard. He hurried toward the tree, and a robin pulling at a fat worm flew off in alarm then watched from a safe distance, guarding his prize.

Brick knelt beside the tree and plucked the bit of yellow. A daffodil. The first sign of spring. There were three in bloom, and he plucked them all, then went whistling up the walkway.

He eased open the front door, wanting to surprise Helen. Leaving his shoes in the hallway, he crept through the house like a thief, peering around corners and through doorways, looking for his wife.

Usually she was downstairs this time of day, either in the sun room relaxing with a cup of tea or curled on the sofa with a good book. Always there was the music. Both of them loved music, especially blues, jazz, and classical, and they kept a stack of CDs on the stereo at all times.

Today Helen was playing Ravel. "Bolero." It was loud enough to cover an invasion of killer elephants, but still Brick tiptoed. He loved surprising Helen, loved the wide-eyed look she always got, adored the way her mouth rounded and her cheeks turned pink.

He scouted the entire downstairs before starting up to the second floor. She was in their bedroom, sitting at the antique secretary beside the window. The late-afternoon sun slanted across her hair and her cheeks.

As always, Brick was awestruck by her beauty. How could one man be so lucky? She was not only sweet and kind and talented, but she was the most beautiful woman he'd ever seen. He watched in silence, the spring bouquet hidden behind his back.

In a moment, he would make his presence known. He would call her name, then she'd turn and smile. Her eyes would light up and she'd cross the room to him. Sometimes she hurried and sometimes she deliberately took her time, holding him with her eyes as she made him wait for her. Hurrying or slowly gliding, she was always elegant. Everything she did was elegant, everything she touched.

In a moment he would hold her. Her lips would touch his, and he'd know paradise.

He eased the flowers from behind his back, opened his mouth to call her name. And then he noticed the tension. It was in her stiff back, in the way she held her head, in her slight frown. What in the world was going on? Had someone done something to hurt her?

Slowly she picked up the calendar on the desk. With a pencil she circled the days.

Brick made some quick mental calculations. It was close to Helen's time of the month. Her pencil slowed, then moved back to the top of the calendar.

She was counting the days. Checking to make sure she was not pregnant.

Brick squeezed the stems of the daffodils so hard, their heads drooped. He'd never told her. Something always sidetracked them.

She laid down the calendar, then turned to stare out the window. Her shoulders sagged.

She didn't want his children. She was still scared he'd run away and leave them. Abandon her with a baby, just as three men had abandoned her mother when she was a child.

How could he possibly tell her that he wanted children more than anything in the world, that he'd wanted children from the day he was old enough to understand where they came from. That even in the orphanage he'd wanted to be a part of a family, to grow up and have a family of his own.

He'd meant to discuss it all in New Hampshire

—her fears, his dreams. But they'd always gotten sidetracked.

And now he was afraid to open that subject, afraid to bring any hint of controversy or dissension into a perfect marriage. They had it all— great careers, great friends, and each other.

What more did they need?

He turned on his most charming smile, the one he often used onstage.

"Helen?"

She turned slowly. Her eyes didn't light immediately the way they always did. His heart stood still.

Then she turned on her most charming smile, the one she used to dazzle an audience.

"Brick . . . sweetheart."

Her pencil clattered to the desk as she hurried across the room to him.

"I brought you flowers. Daffodils. The first ones of spring."

He held out the three flowers with their bruised stems and pitiful drooping heads.

"You're sweet." She handled them reverently, as if they were the most expensive of hothouse roses. "Thank you, precious."

"You're welcome, darling."

She hugged him around the waist, squeezing so hard, he could feel her arms tremble. He glanced across the room at the calendar on top of the desk. Was his wife pregnant? Did she carry his child?

"Helen . . ."

Slowly she lifted her face to his. Was that the track of tears on her cheeks?

"Yes?"

Tenderly he placed one hand on her cheek. He couldn't bear to hurt her. In the face of her obvious fear, he couldn't bear to say, "I want a child."

Pick a safe subject. Anything.

"Angelica wants us to do a reprise of *The Taming of the Shrew.*"

"Where?"

"Philadelphia."

"When?"

"The beginning of next month."

"What did you tell her?"

"That I'd discuss it with you." He kissed the top of her head, her brow, her cheekbones. "What do you say, beautiful? Ready to be tamed again by your husband?"

She leaned back in his arms, her old sassiness almost restored.

"You can do the taming onstage," she said. "I'll do it offstage."

"Do you promise to use those scarlet ribbons?"

"I promise."

"It's a deal, darling."

"Good." Her smile was real this time.

"Let's seal it."

"Anything in mind?"

"I was thinking about a game . . . of gin rummy."

"I was thinking about another game . . . with orange slices and grapes."

"What? No strawberries?"

"You want it all, don't you, Brick Sullivan?"

"Indeed I do, Helen Sullivan."

"Why don't you get comfortable while I go down to the kitchen and get the fruit?"

"I like the way you think, darling."

He stood and watched until she was out of the room and down the stairs; then he hurried to the desk and picked up the calendar. Thirty-three days. Helen was late.

Jubilation filled him, then terror. His hands shook as he unbuttoned his shirt. He tossed it toward the armchair and missed. He kicked off his shoes and stripped off his socks any old way, then left his pants where they fell.

A trail of clothes led to the bed. Stretched out, he tried to relax.

But relaxation was impossible. Disgusted, he left the bed and paced the floor. His mind was a jumble of things he should have said, things he should have done before the wedding. Before they'd left New Hampshire. Before they'd settled into the house in Georgia.

He balled one hand into a fist and smashed it into his palm. He was caught again in a web of his own making, a pretense. Brick and Helen Sullivan. The perfect couple. The perfect marriage. The perfect partners, onstage and off.

It was true. Almost.

Brick was disgusted with himself. He paced to the window, then back to the bed.

The bed. He wouldn't think of anything right now except his wife in the kitchen, slicing fresh fruit.

Already he could smell the oranges, taste the juice as it trickled slowly over her body, taste the sweet nectar of Helen's skin.

"Hurry, my darling," he whispered. He needed to drown his fears in her.

Helen pressed against the kitchen counter and leaned her head against the cabinet. What in the world would she do if she was pregnant?

She pressed her hands flat across her womb as if it already contained her child, as if she were protecting it from all harm.

Scenes from their stay in New Hampshire played through her mind. Onstage during re-hearsals she'd told Brick that more than anything she'd wanted his child. What had his response been?

She squeezed her eyes shut, trying to remember his exact words. There were none to remember. They'd gotten into a silly argument about little girls wearing frilly dresses to the park.

But he had never said, "I want children."

What if he didn't? He'd said he wouldn't leave her if she had a child, but had he really meant it?

Heavy with uncertainty, Helen got the sliced oranges, then arranged them on a tray with grapes and strawberries. She couldn't bear to discuss the subject of children with Brick, couldn't bear to bring up a subject that might mar and even destroy their happiness.

She squeezed her eyes shut, then wiped away the tear that trickled onto her cheek. Leaning over, she looked at her reflection in the shiny tray. She didn't want any sign of crying to show. She could see none, but just to be certain she rubbed her cheeks until they were pink.

Then she went upstairs with the tray. Smiling. Always smiling.

Brick heard her coming up the stairs. He hurried to the bed, then sprawled out with his hands above his head.

No. That looked too posed.

He stretched out his arms as if he were lounging in a deck chair beside the pool, soaking up the sun. Much better. More relaxed looking.

"Sweetheart?"

She stood in the doorway with her tray full of fresh fruit. Smiling.

He propped on one elbow and grinned at her.

"Mrs. Sullivan, I'd say you have on too many clothes."

"What do you plan to do about it, Mr. Sullivan?"

He arranged his face into ferocious lines, then got up and stalked her.

"The beast plans to devour the lady."

He lunged at her, but she sidestepped.

"No." Laughing, she began to stalk him. "The lady is going to devour the beast, bit by bit, saving the best parts till last."

"What are the best parts?"

She nibbled his ears, his neck, his lips.

"Hmmm. I don't know. I haven't tasted them all. But the ones I've tasted so far have been delicious."

She focused her attention on his mouth once more. He reached for her zipper with one hand and a slice of orange with the other.

He heard her leave the bed before dawn. She was moving cautiously, as if she didn't want to wake him.

Brick lay perfectly still, letting her carry on her charade. The bathroom door opened, and she slipped inside. He listened to the sounds, cabinet door opening, water running, toilet flushing, crying.

Crying?

He started to bolt from the bed, and then he settled back against the pillow, tense. She'd been so careful not to wake him. That meant she wanted to be alone.

It was a clear spring night. The pale light of predawn poured through the French doors. As his eyes adjusted, Brick saw Helen's silk robe hanging on the end of the bed. She was usually so elegant, so organized that even when she went to the bathroom in the middle of the night she slipped into her robe.

Her sobs were soft, indistinct, as if she were trying to muffle them. Helen never cried.

What could be the problem? He'd allow her a few more minutes of privacy, and if she didn't come out, he'd go in to see about her.

Helen's robe took on a rosy glow as the light changed from gray to pink. The fragrance of tea roses drifted up from her pillow.

Brick rolled to her side of the bed, and that's when he saw it . . . a pale stain on the sheets, a sign that his wife was not pregnant.

Helen was crying with relief because she wasn't carrying his baby. For a moment, his heart hurt so much that he thought he would cry. Then he rolled back to his side of the bed and pretended to be asleep.

Reporters from all over the nation had gathered in Philadelphia to watch the Sullivans reprise their roles of Petruchio and Kate in *The Taming of the Shrew*. Brick and Helen faced a battery of lights and cameras, their faces arranged in their famous stage smiles.

The questions came at them hot and heavy.

"Will you do the play as Shakespeare wrote it or as you rewrote it in New Hampshire?"

Helen deferred to Brick, smiling.

"Straight Shakespeare this time. Helen and I ad-libbed the play in New Hampshire to fit the occasion." He reached for his wife's hand. "Since the *occasion* took this time, we see no need to repeat that performance. Ever."

There was general laughter from the reporters.

"Do you plan to do all your plays together?"

Helen laughed. "Brick is not only the greatest Shakespearean actor of our time but is also my favorite leading man. We'll do as many plays as we can together, but no, we won't do everything as a team. Both of us will accept solo engagements."

"What's next after *The Taming of the Shrew?*"

"*Much Ado About Nothing* in Dallas," Brick said.

"Together?"

"Yes . . ." he added. "Together."

"Do you plan to have children to carry on the acting tradition of the Sullivans?"

Helen's hand trembled in his, but her smile held. He kept his too.

"No comment," he said.

The reporters, sensing a real story, wouldn't let it alone.

"Helen, if you do have children, will you retire from the theater?"

"No comment." She kept her voice even, her smile intact.

"Brick, if you have children, will *you* retire?" This from a female reporter.

"No comment."

He and Helen stood up, signaling an end to the interview.

"Just one more question . . ."

"Sorry. Helen and I have to get ready for the matinee performance."

He studied his wife as they ducked out. She was as tightly wound as a revival preacher who had faced down a church full of sinners.

Now that the subject had been broached, it would be a good time for the two of them to discuss children. *Are you afraid to have my baby, Helen? Afraid I'll run?*

As they hurried toward their dressing rooms, the stage manager called out, "Thirty minutes to curtain, Brick."

Thirty minutes was barely time to get into makeup and costume.

The subject of children would have to wait.

FOURTEEN

The thunder of applause roared around them. Helen and Brick took their vows hand in hand as they always did. Before the curtain rang down for the last time, Brick kissed Helen in full view of the delighted audience as he always did.

Philadelphia. Dallas. Chicago. San Francisco. Washington, D.C.

It was always the same. Rehearse. Perform. Take a whirlwind break, filling whatever little time they allowed themselves with a marathon of loving.

No late-night conversations, no soul-baring discussions. There was never any time for that.

It was almost as if they were both sailors drowning at sea, and the only lifeboat available to them was the solid, unsinkable one formed when their bodies joined and their hearts and souls and minds merged.

Helen lost track of the time, lost track of the cities.

Where were they now? D.C. She remembered because they could see the Washington Monument outside their hotel window.

The audience applauded in wild appreciation as Brick kissed her. Still holding her tightly, he whispered in her ear.

"What do you say we blow this joint, baby, and go where we can really let our hair down?"

"How about the zoo?"

The curtain rang down, and the actors milled around them, calling congratulations to one another, making plans to meet next day for lunch or next week to discuss doing a project together, or next month in New York—plans they would never carry out.

"The zoo?" Brick arched one eyebrow at her, grinning wickedly. "You're talking my kind of language. Kinky sex among the wild beasts. It's closed, but maybe we can scale the fence."

"I want to see the pandas."

He cupped her face and held it very still for his inspection.

"You're serious, aren't you?"

"Yes."

They stood that way for a long time, Brick searching her face and Helen searching his.

Tell him, she thought. *Tell him you want children.*

He was a wonderful man, intelligent, kind, af-

fectionate, passionate, trustworthy, witty, fun loving. Why couldn't she bring herself to broach the
subject closest to her heart?

Because she wasn't sure where it would lead
them. That was why.

And she was scared.

Putting on a bright smile that she hoped he
wouldn't see was forced, she stood on tiptoe and
kissed him.

"Hmmm. I like that," he said.

"The pandas can wait."

Holding his hand, she raced with him toward
their dressing room. They left a trail of clothes
across the stage, in the wings, up the short flight
of stairs, and down the narrow hallway.

By the time they got to their dressing room,
they barely had on enough to be considered de-
cent.

"Good thing nobody was around to see us,"
she whispered, already in his arms.

"Would it have made any difference to us?"
He lifted her hips, wrapped her legs around him,
and braced her against the wall.

His heat already invaded her, just as his body
soon would. Limp with desire, she leaned her
head against the wall.

"You're protected?" he whispered.

Helen bit down on her lip. Even in their most
passionate moments, even when she was close to
screaming with need, even with his hard heat al-

ready pushing against her cleft, he never forgot to ask.

There would be no unwanted children for Brick Sullivan.

"Yes," she said.

His thrust was so deep, she arched like a fish. Impaled. Hooked. Reeled with expert finesse through the dark, stormy seas till she was brought at last to the surface, gasping.

Limp, she wrapped her arms around him, and he carried her to the daybed. They lay tangled together in sweet abandon, napping, occasionally waking to whisper love words, then drifting to sleep until passion overtook them once more.

They made slow, dreamy love in the cramped dressing room of the deserted theater, not caring that a perfectly good bed had gone to waste back at their hotel room.

They had each other, and nothing else mattered.

Brick kissed her cheek and tenderly smoothed her hair back from her face.

"Tears, Helen?"

"It's nothing. Just exhaustion."

He kissed the dampness away, then held her close with his head resting in her hair.

"Tomorrow we'll take the day off and go see the bears," he said.

"Pandas."

He laughed. "We'll see the whole damned zoo."

"I see one." Helen grabbed Brick's arm, point-ing. "Look. Do you see him?"

"Where?"

"Over there. That little patch of black."

"That's the tree trunk, Helen."

"Oh."

She sounded as disappointed as a little girl. Looked it too. Her hair was pulled up in a ponytail, the end sticking through a baseball cap, and she wore no makeup. She wore denim shorts and a T-shirt that said, Everybody has to kiss a few frogs before they find a prince.

She'd kissed him, all right. But had he turned into a prince?

Right now, he felt like a heel. The sun was shining, the weather was beautiful, Helen was happy, and all he could think of was how he'd feel if he had children tugging on his hands saying, "Lift me up, Daddy, I want to see the panda bears."

He glanced around him. There were children everywhere—a little boy in overalls racing with his sister, a cherub with a pink face and yellow corkscrew curls crying over her spilled cotton candy, a devilish urchin with freckles and a cow-lick trying to kick an empty soda can with every step he took.

A vast emptiness overtook him.

"Look, Brick." Helen grabbed his arm. "Over there. I'm sure that's him."

It was not one of the pandas, but the movement of a tree limb.

"Do you see him?" she said, her face filled with happy anticipation.

"Yes. I see him."

She was so lovely, so trusting, so wonderful. What was the harm of one more lie?

The smell of gardenia was overwhelming. Brick paused on the brick walkway to enjoy the sweet smell of summer.

At least, that was the reason he gave himself for pausing. The real reason was tucked under his arm, the script for a new off-Broadway production that went into rehearsals the next week. He would play the lead, a man plunged in darkness, stripped of pride by war and illness, fighting his way back to the light.

It was a great role for him, a chance to spread his wings, try something new.

But there was nothing for Helen in the play.

He didn't ease open the front door as was his habit, then tiptoe through the house so he could surprise her. Instead he made a bold and noisy entrance.

"I'm home," he called.

"In here."

She was sitting in the sun room with her yellow skirts spread out around her and her hair loose over her shoulders.

"You look like a daffodil." He kissed her lips. "Hmm. Taste like a rose."

Usually she had a snappy comeback. Today she merely smiled and caressed his cheek.

The script under his arm felt like a betrayal.

"I'm having iced tea," she said. "Do you want some?"

"Yes. Tea sounds good."

Hairs prickled along the back of his neck. She was so still, so reserved. Pulling back his chair, he studied her face. She was thinner. When had she lost weight and why hadn't he noticed?

She'd been working too hard. Maybe the script under his arm wasn't a betrayal at all but a salvation. Helen needed to take a break, to stay at home and soak up the sun beside the pool, to walk in the sunshine and eat ice cream, to loll on the patio, reading a good book and listening to great music.

Helen handed him a glass from the tray, and he reached for the pitcher of iced tea. That's when he saw the script lying on the glass-topped table— *The Glass Menagerie*.

He glanced from the script to Helen. Her face flushed, and she brushed her hair back from her forehead, a gesture she used only when she was flustered.

"I was thinking about doing something different for a while," she said. "Laura Wingfield."

"It's a great role."

"It's in Houston."

"Houston should be nice this time of year."

She toyed with her glass. He ignored his tea.

"You could come," she said.

"When?"

"Rehearsals start the day after tomorrow."

So soon. She must have known for a while. Why hadn't she told him?

"Actually, I was thinking of doing something different myself."

He pulled the script from under his arm and laid it on the table. Helen picked it up and studied it.

"It looks interesting. Just the kind of role to showcase your talents." She laid his script back on the table beside hers.

"I'm glad you think so."

They both picked up their glasses and pretended to drink tea.

"When do you start rehearsals?" she asked.

"Next week."

"Hmmm." She thumbed through her script, ruffling the pages back and forth. "This might be good for us, you know? Taking solo roles. We're so accustomed to each other, perhaps we're getting stale." Her cheeks colored. "Onstage, I mean."

"I knew what you meant."

Cold winds of fear blew across his soul. She was leaving in two days. Once she was out there in

Houston, Texas, would she decide not to come back?

Lifting his glass, he studied his wife over the rim. Her eyes were lowered, the eyelashes fanning across her porcelain cheeks, a lovely blush covering her face, her lips moist from the tea and slightly parted.

No force in heaven or on earth could ever take her away from him again.

"Helen . . ."

She glanced up, her eyes riveted on his. There was a crash as his chair fell over backward, then a blur of yellow and a rending noise as he pushed aside her skirts and tore the wisp of silk. In one swift move he lifted her onto the edge of the table and entered her. The tea tray went skittering away and crashed to the floor. Their glasses tipped over and ice cubes clattered around the glass tabletop.

Theirs was the wild mating of two desperate people, the kind of love that sought to obliterate everything except their bodies and the many ways they could use them to please each other. Buttons made small pinging noises against the glass as Helen tore his shirt open. Her eyes never left Brick's as she reached blindly for an ice cube. She brought it dripping to the bodice of her dress. Riveted he watched her rub the ice around her nipples.

It made a dark, wet circle on the yellow fabric.

Passion exploded through him. The table threatened to turn over.

Still joined, he eased her to the floor. Leaning over, he circled his tongue around the wet fabric, then pulled her nipple in his mouth, suckling deeply. She spasmed again and again.

She brought the nearly melted ice cube to his chest, traced a line from his throat to his navel. Wild with need, drunk with hunger, they rolled around the floor, changing positions. She licked the small, cool trail of water off his chest, using the long sweeping movements of some fine jungle cat grooming her mate.

Her skirt became entangled in their legs. Impatient, she jerked it aside, ripping the fabric. Brick tore the rest of the skirt away, then caught her hips to his. Holding her tightly, he thrust upward, high and hard. She arched, her head falling back to expose her smooth throat. They were champion thoroughbreds racing for the finish line, their bodies lathered and their hearts pumping so hard, they almost burst.

They reached the end of the race at the same time, their cries of release mingling as she received his seed. Afterward, they lay together a long time, their hearts pounding and their breathing ragged.

Finally he lifted himself on his elbows and looked around the room. The torn yellow skirt lay among spilled tea, melted ice, and bits of broken glass.

His gaze shifted to Helen. She had the usual flushed look of a woman well loved, but there was something about her eyes that made his heart stand still. They were shattered, distant, as if they were already seeing things he could not see.

"I guess we'd better clean up this mess," he said.

"It looks like a battleground," she whispered.

Fear began to close in on him.

Perhaps it was.

FIFTEEN

Helen was late for the wedding.

Brick scanned the crowd, searching for the familiar dark hair, the tall regal body, the exquisite face. The church pews were filled with people who had come to see Matt Rider and Barb Gladly exchange vows, but Helen Sullivan was nowhere in sight.

Up front, the minister intoned the vows, "Do you take this woman . . ."

There was a flurry across the aisle from Brick as Helen slid into the pew. He felt as if he'd been kicked in the gut. She was even more beautiful than he remembered, even more desirable. She glowed, as if candles had been lit just underneath her skin.

Their gazes met, touched, held.

Why had he ever agreed to anything that would take him away from her for two weeks? An eternity.

She turned her attention to the front of the church, but he made no pretense of caring what was going on at the altar. He had eyes only for his wife.

The ceremony seemed endless, the procession drawn out. Brick's only thought was getting out of the crowd and getting close to his wife.

By the time the wedding procession had filed out of the church, Helen was caught up in the milling crowd and being propelled out of his sight. There was no way he could get to her short of mowing down several people and leaving them flat on the floor. Even Brick was not bold enough to do that.

The wedding party had dispersed to the fellowship hall, where champagne flowed freely and cake was being urged on the guests by overanxious women teetering on shoes that made them walk as if they were balancing on a high wire.

Helen was in the inner circle that surrounded the bride and groom. Brick refused the glass that was being shoved into his hand and made his way toward her.

She was standing to the left and slightly back of Barb, trying not to steal the limelight. She spotted him when he was halfway across the room. Her eyes never left his.

"Hello, Brick." Although he was the one who had been hurrying, she was the one who sounded breathless.

"Helen." He touched her arm, leaned to kiss

her lightly on the mouth. What he wanted to do was sweep her into his arms and run with her, run so fast and so far that there would be no theaters to beckon either of them, no reporters to hound them with probing questions.

But this was Matt and Barb's day. He would do nothing to take attention away from them.

His need for Helen was so great that he felt certain the wedding guests could see the sparks flying. He kept his hold on her arm, not merely a small contact but as a claim.

This woman is mine.

He felt the tremor that ran through her. Was she? Was she still his?

Matt's friends were regaling him with tales of their own *awful* wedded bliss.

"Just wait till you have that first argument. Man, you'll wish her aunt Tilda had never given her a rolling pin."

"Wait till she cooks her first meal."

"It's best not to live close to her mother. Martha ran away to her mother at least six times."

"Six times the first year?" Matt asked.

"Naw. Six times the first day."

Brick and Helen politely joined the general laughter, and patiently waited their turn to offer congratulations.

"Yeah, Matt, and just wait till the babies start coming. All you have to look forward to in the middle of the night is dirty diapers."

The speaker was a close personal friend of

Matt's, Glenn Houser, a body trainer who had often visited Matt in the Sullivan gym. His face lit up when he spotted Brick and Helen.

"Hey, man." He pounded Brick on the back and caught Helen's hand in an iron grip. "Look, everybody, the Sullivans. Now there's a man too smart to saddle himself with kids." He pounded Brick on the back. "Right, man?"

"Right." Brick's response was automatic, a quick and easy way out of an awkward situation.

Helen stiffened.

He tried to catch her eye, but she moved between Matt and Barb, wrapped her arms around them, and began to chat.

Brick waited.

Helen delayed.

In less than an hour both of them would be flying out, going their separate ways, hurrying so they wouldn't miss their curtain calls.

Finally there was no graceful way Helen could stay wedged between the newlyweds.

"Come with me." Brick took her arm and led her through the crowd.

"Where are you taking me? I have a plane to catch."

"I don't give a damn about planes. I need to see you."

"You have a curtain call."

"I don't give a damn about curtain calls."

He found a small empty hallway. Pulling her into his arms, he leaned against the wall.

"That's better," he said. "Isn't that better, Helen?"

"Yes." Her voice was muffled against his shirt.

Suddenly he was kissing her hungrily, desperately, as if he were a soldier returned from the war. There was so much he needed to say, so much he needed to hear. But his need to hold her, to touch her, to kiss her overrode all others.

They clung together, devouring each other, wanting more. Finally they had to come up for breath.

"I wish you didn't have to fly back, Helen. Can you change your plans?"

"Can you?"

He had never missed opening night. Not even for sickness. It wasn't fair to the people who had paid to see him.

"No," he said.

"Neither can I."

"We have to take some time, Helen. Soon."

"Yes. Soon."

Why did her *soon* sound like *never?* The separation was making Brick paranoid.

"My plane leaves soon. Let's not waste a minute."

He crushed her mouth under his once more, drowning out everything except his need.

Sunlight poured through the hotel windows and fell across the suitcases open on the bed.

Trails of lingerie crisscrossed the room, a jumble of blouses waited to be organized, and jewelry glittered like stars across the bedspread.

It was the same scene she'd played over and over the last few weeks, and for a moment Helen couldn't remember whether she was packing or unpacking, whether she was in Dallas or Boston or Chicago.

The hotel suites all looked alike—clean modern furniture, innocuous pictures on the wall, coordinated colors.

Sterile. Comfortless. Empty.

Marsha bustled in from the sitting room, took one look at the mess, shook her head, and began to organize the packing.

Dear Marsha. What would Helen ever do without her?

Tears clogged the back of Helen's throat. She tried to swallow them, but they wouldn't go down. Besides that, her knees felt rubbery and her head hurt.

Tired of being strong, sick of putting on a front, she sank to the middle of the floor and wailed like a homesick puppy.

Marsha went into the bathroom and came back with a handful of tissues; then she went about packing and let Helen have her cry.

Helen dabbed at her eyes, sniffing.

"I don't know what's wrong with me."

"I do."

"I suppose you're going to tell me."

"If you'd asked me in the first place, we wouldn't be here. We'd be at home sitting in the sunshine instead of trying to avoid being mugged every time we step out on the streets. And we for sure wouldn't be fixing to traipse off to some other godforsaken city so you can wear yourself ragged up on a stage."

"That's what I do, Marsha. I'm an actress."

"You're a married actress. If you ask me, this is no way to conduct a marriage." Marsha straightened a stack of skirts, shaking them out so hard, the fabric made snapping noises.

"Brick understands. He's an actor."

"He's a man. I don't claim to be an expert on this subject, Lord knows, ornery old cuss that I am. But I figure a man like Brick Sullivan needs a woman in his bed."

"He would never betray me."

"I didn't say he would, didn't even *think* it. I said he needs a woman in his bed." She shook out a blouse with unnecessary vigor. "And I'm wondering how come it's been so long since you've been there. Not that it's any of my business."

"Eight weeks is not a long time to be on the road."

"Balderdash."

"You don't have to go with me to Seattle, Marsha. I can manage fine on my own."

"You can't find your way out of a paper sack on your own. You may be brilliant on the stage, but when it comes to dealing with practical matters, you're a babe in the woods."

"You're too go..ood to me."

A fresh gale of tears overtook her, and she padded to the bathroom to get some more tissue. When she got back Marsha was posed with arms akimbo and that I'm-not-taking-any-more-of-this-nonsense look on her face.

"Look at you," Marsha said. "You're worn to a frazzle. What I want to know is how come it's so all-fired important to do that play in Seattle. Why don't you take a break? Go home and be with Brick for a few weeks."

"Brick's not home. He's in New Yo..ork."

Helen broke down once more. Alarmed, Marsha went into the bathroom and got a wet cloth for her face.

"You're going to make yourself sick with all this crying." She washed Helen's face, then made her lie on the bed with the washcloth over her forehead. "You may already be sick."

"I do have a headache."

"I don't wonder, with all this flitting around from pillar to post. I'll bet you don't even know what day it is."

"Sunday." Helen gave her a rueful grin. "I only know because I did my last performance tonight."

"Sunday the what?"

"Eighteenth? Twenty-fifth?"

"See . . . You're working so hard, you don't even know the date. What you need is a break."

"I promise I'll take a break soon, Marsha."

"When?"

Helen pressed the cloth to her head. It was a good question. One she couldn't even answer herself. The last time she'd tried to arrange a break, Brick had been tied up in Boston. Then when he'd tried to arrange for them to meet, she'd had to stay over in Tampa.

They'd joked about it on the phone.

"Guess you've already forgotten what I look like," he'd said when their plans to meet in Jackson Hole had been canceled.

"You've probably found a new leading lady," she'd joked when their plans to meet back home for a few days had been ditched because of conflicting schedules.

But was it their schedules that kept them apart? Or was it something else?

A vivid mental picture of Brick at Matt's wedding came to her.

Helen didn't even want to think about that right now. All she wanted to do was ease her headache.

"As soon as I do the next show, Marsha," she said.

Or maybe the next. Or the next.

❖───────❖

Angelica had never seen Brick so still. He sat on the sofa trying to look relaxed with his feet stretched out on the coffee table, but she knew better. His body was stiff as a poker.

"I've decided to do *Macbeth* in Boston," he said.

"What about Helen? Will she do Lady Macbeth?"

There was a quick flash of something in his eyes, something Angelica couldn't read. But she knew him well enough to guess, knew both of them.

There was trouble in paradise. And she didn't like it. Not one little bit.

"No. She's going to be in San Francisco. Or is it Seattle?"

"You don't even know where your own wife is." It was not a question but a statement. Angelica stood, smoothing down her skirt. She perched on the front of her desk and fixed him with a motherly look. "I'm just going to say this once, Brick."

"Perhaps you shouldn't say it at all. I don't like the look on your face."

"I don't have a look on my face."

"Yes, you do. It's your cross between Godzilla and Mother Teresa."

"Gee, thanks."

"You're welcome." He quirked one eyebrow at her and treated her to his famous grin.

"I won't be sidetracked by your charm."

"Am I charming?"

"Millions of people think you are. At the moment I think you're foolish."

"Is that a personal opinion or a professional one?"

"Furthermore, I think you're running scared."

"I'm not scared of the devil."

"What about your wife? Are you scared of her?"

Brick left the sofa and stalked to the window. Angelica had hit a nerve. Ramming his hands deep into his pockets, he looked out over the city. Summertime in New York.

And Helen was . . . Angelica was right: He didn't even know where his own wife was.

"Maybe I am, Angelica . . . but I don't seem to know what to do about it." He turned back from the window. "Any ideas?"

Angelica was as pleased as if he'd given her a priceless gift. She'd always felt maternal toward Brick. She knew his background, knew he had grown up in an orphanage, knew he had no one to turn to for motherly advice. It pleased her to think that he would turn to her. It even made up for all the emptiness in her own life, the fiancé that somehow never got around to taking her down the aisle, the empty years of waiting for somebody else to come along, the sudden realization that even if he did, she was too old for children.

"Why don't you hold off on accepting *Macbeth?* Take some time off. Call Helen and ask her to do the same thing."

Brick stood with his hands in his pockets, rocking back and forth on his heels.

"Well?" Angelica said.

"Damned if I'm not scared. What do you suppose that means?"

"I think it's a good sign."

"Of what?"

"That I'm right."

He grinned. "I guess you want to celebrate with champagne."

"I can't think of a better occasion. I'll go get the bottle."

While she was gone, Brick stared out the window. He knew she was right. He and Helen couldn't spend the rest of their lives onstage in different cities. He had to see her again. *Needed* to see her.

But what if she didn't want to see him?

As soon as he got back to his hotel he took down Helen's itinerary. Looking at her schedule, he realized that something was dreadfully wrong with a marriage when a husband had to have an itinerary to locate his wife.

Picking up the phone, he dialed her hotel in Seattle. She'd be checking in late that night.

"This is Brick Sullivan. I'd like to leave a message for . . ."

"Sir? Who is the message for?"

He didn't want to converse with his wife via

messenger; he wanted to do it personally. Suddenly it occurred to Brick how very much he wanted to see his wife, how very foolish he had been to stay away all this time.

"No one," he said. "No messages."

What he had to say could only be said in person.

Helen had never been airsick before. And the plane wasn't even off the ground. It sat on the runway, held by thunderstorms that swept through Dallas.

Locked in the tiny bathroom on the plane, she bent over the toilet, her face sweaty and her stomach heaving.

Maybe Marsha was right. Maybe she needed a break.

She ran water over a paper towel and pressed it to her face and neck, then returned to her seat.

"Are you okay?" Marsha squeezed her hand.

"I'm fine . . . Don't give me that look. It's lack of sleep, that's all."

The plane taxied slowly behind a long line of jets awaiting takeoff. The intercom crackled, and the pilot came on the air.

"Another short delay, folks. Sorry about that. We should be taking off in another hour."

"Hmph. He said that two hours ago. Why we can't just go back to the terminal and . . ."

Marsha was suddenly talking to thin air as Helen raced back toward the toilet.

Helen leaned against the tiny sink, splashing water on her face. Dripping, she came up and stared at herself in the wavery mirror. She looked like a ghost. And she felt even worse. She was so tired.

How long had she been on the road? Eight weeks. It was enough to make anybody tired.

Eight weeks since she'd seen Brick, not counting the brief encounter at Matt's wedding. Eight weeks since they'd shared a home, a meal, a bed. Eight weeks . . .

Helen pressed her hands over her abdomen. She was pregnant. She didn't need early pregnancy tests and doctors to tell her. She *knew*. She was going to have a baby.

Joy filled her. A baby. A little girl who would wear frilly dresses and pink hair ribbons. A little angel who would have tea parties in the backyard and impromptu piano recitals in the den. A little doll with her long legs and Brick's black eyes.

Brick. Helen groaned. How would she ever tell Brick?

She saw him as he had been at Matt's wedding, the quick smile, the easy charm, the carefree manner.

Brick's too smart to saddle himself with children, right?

Right, Brick had said.

A wave of nausea hit Helen once more, and she bent over the toilet, heaving. When the sickness passed, she wrapped her arms protectively around her abdomen and leaned against the wall.

What was she going to do?

SIXTEEN

Brick paced the airport like a crazy man. Chance had put him in Seattle before Helen—chance and bad weather.

Thunderstorms. He didn't want to think of Helen caught in a plane in a thunderstorm.

Think of something else.

Think of what he would say to her when he saw her. This time he had to do it right. No more postponing. No more getting sidetracked. No more running.

He checked the monitor for the hundredth time. Helen's plane was finally scheduled for arrival. He had time for a quick snack before she was due to land.

Sitting at a cramped table with the soup and sandwich he'd ordered, he realized he couldn't possibly eat. How could he eat when his stomach was tied in knots?

He dumped the food in the garbage can and

made his way toward her gate. A huge crowd had lined up to meet the plane. Brick tried to get closer, but short of stepping over bodies, there was nothing he could do except hang around at the back of the crowd.

A cheer went up from the crowd when the jet from Dallas landed. Brick watched over the heads of the crowd as passengers began to deplane. He saw Marsha first, and then Helen.

"Helen," he called to her, waving to attract her attention.

She didn't see him. He tried to get through the crush of people but forward movement was impossible.

Craning his neck to see her over the crowd, Brick began a lateral movement that would put him on a collision course with his wife.

She looked pale from her long ordeal on the plane. She was thinner too. He knew Helen. Sometimes when she was on the road she didn't take the time to eat properly.

He should have been at her side, taking care of her. What kind of husband paraded around onstage in strange cities while his wife got pale and thin?

She was coming out of the crowd now, headed for the baggage claim.

"Helen!"

Her head jerked around. She went even paler. There was no welcome smile on her face, no welcome light in her eyes.

For a moment he wasn't certain she would even stop. Fear mingled with joy as he hurried toward her. She clutched her carryon bag as if it were a life raft.

"Brick . . . what are you doing in Seattle?"

"I came to see my wife." She was stiff in his embrace. And damned if she didn't offer her cheek instead of her lips.

Wounded pride replaced both joy and fear.

"Happy to see me, Helen?"

"Surprised."

She pulled out of his embrace and moved toward the escalators that would take them down to the baggage claim area. He fell into step beside her.

"You don't have to go with me. Marsha and I can manage this."

"I'm going."

"Suit yourself."

Marsha rolled her eyes but kept her silence. That was the thing he'd always admired about her; she never butted in, never took sides.

They lined up on the escalators, Marsha in front, Helen behind her, then Brick. His wife's shoulders were as stiff as if they'd been set in concrete.

What in the devil was going on? Hadn't he flown all the way across country to find out?

"Why don't we find a quiet place where we can sit down for a minute and talk, Helen?"

"I need to get my bags so I can check into the hotel. I'm tired."

"Why don't you and Marsha go directly there. I'll take care of the bags and join you later."

"You're booked at our hotel?"

That did it.

"Am I booked at your hotel!"

"You needn't shout. I'm not deaf."

Heads began to turn in their direction. Someone in the crowd shouted, "It's Brick and Helen Sullivan," and a small crowd began to gather at the foot of the escalator.

"I realize that old saying about absence making the heart grow fonder is a bunch of hogwash, but I didn't think my own wife would turn me out after only eight weeks."

"You're making a scene." The only sign Helen showed that she was irritated was a slight frown.

"You're my wife, for Pete's sake. I think you're worth making a scene over."

"Can't we discuss this later, Brick?"

"When? Next week? Next month? Next year?"

The escalator malfunctioned and ground to a stop. Neither of them noticed.

Helen turned her back and stoically faced forward. He caught her shoulders and forced her to look at him.

"When, Helen?"

"Not now, Brick. I have a headache."

Helen had never acted this way before, not

even when she'd left him at the end of a five-year marriage. Brick began to panic. Logic fled.

"I won't be shut out, Helen. Not now. Not ever again." Her bottom lip trembled, and she caught it between her teeth. If Brick hadn't been in such a state of panic, he'd have crumbled at that small sign of Helen's distress.

He was like a snowball on a downhill roll; he'd gotten off to a bad start at the beginning, and now there was no way he could keep himself from crashing into everything in his path.

"Helen, you put me off at Matt's wedding . . ."

"*I* put *you* off?"

"You wouldn't change your plans."

"*I* wouldn't change plans? What about you? You wouldn't change your precious plans either."

"The important thing—"

"Yes, Brick. Let's talk about the important thing." Her face flushed, and she brushed a lock of hair out of her face. "The important thing is that you told that . . . that *gorilla* that you were too smart to have children."

"You're the one who's always been too scared to have children, Helen. Not me. I always wanted children . . ."

"You did?"

"Yes. But I don't have to have them to make my life complete, Helen. I have you, and that's all that matters." Her lip trembled in earnest now, and a tiny tear eased out of the corner of her eye. Brick was too overwrought to notice.

"It's not all that matters," she said.

"Yes, it is. Let's leave children out of this . . ."

"I can't."

"You can if you want to, Helen."

Tears streamed down her cheeks now. Silently, Marsha passed her a tissue.

"I'm afraid not, Brick. It's too late."

"Helen, don't be . . ." Comprehension dawned slowly but surely. Brick studied his wife's tear-streaked face. The light of love he'd looked for earlier was now shining in her eyes. "You're *pregnant?*"

Ever the actor, his awed stage whisper carried to the crowd waiting at the bottom of the stalled escalator.

"Helen Sullivan is going to have a baby," someone yelled.

The rest of the crowd took up the cry.

"Brick and Helen Sullivan are pregnant."

"Do you think it will be a boy or a girl?"

"Do you think they'll let it act?"

"What do you think they'll name it?"

Marsha pulled out another tissue, but she didn't hand it to Helen. She used it to wipe her own eyes.

"Glory be," she said. And then as Brick caught his wife in a tight embrace, "The saints be praised."

"Why didn't you tell me sooner, darling?" Brick murmured against his wife's lips.

"I just found out myself."

"Are you happy, Helen?"

"Ecstatic . . . now that I know you want her too."

"Her?"

"The baby. I'm going to dress her in pink and stroll her around the neighborhood in a pram with a ruffled top."

"It's going to be a boy. And no son of mine is ever going to ride in a pram with ruffles."

"It's not a boy."

"How do you know?"

"Because I've decided to have a girl first."

He pulled her so close, she lost her breath. Bending her over backward, he pressed his lips to her throat.

"First?" he whispered.

"We're going to have lots of babies."

"Don't you think we ought to get started, darling?"

"I think we already did."

As the power came back on, his lips closed over hers, and they rode the escalator toward the cheering audience. When they reached the bottom, Brick Sullivan scooped his favorite leading lady into his arms and took a bow.

"Encore," somebody in the audience said.

His lips closed over Helen's once more.

"With pleasure," he said. "Always."

EPILOGUE

"Would you look at that little smile, Brick? I think she already knows me. Don't you, darling? Don't you already know your mother? Yes, you do."

Helen and her daughter were both dressed in pink. Pink roses filled her hospital room and a pink rose corsage was pinned to her pillow. She leaned over the tiny pink bundle in her arms, cooing.

Brick was so full of pride and love, he thought his heart would burst. Standing at the window, he drank in the sight of his wife and daughter.

A family. After all these years he had a family of his own.

A tiny enraged person let out a big squall, and Helen glanced at Brick in alarm.

"He wants his mother," she said.

"How do you know?"

"I can tell."

Brick smiled down at the tiny blue bundle in his arms.

"Listen to that voice projection," he said. "My son will soon be ready to play Macbeth."

"John's not practicing oratory. He's hungry."

Smiling, Brick placed his son at Helen's breast, then picked up his daughter.

"How's Daddy's little girl? How's my little Jennifer?" The baby's tiny hand closed around Brick's finger. "Look at that, Helen. She knows who her daddy is." He leaned close to coo at his daughter. "Don't you, sweetheart? Don't you know your daddy? Look at that, Helen. She's *smiling.*"

"That's gas."

Brick gave his wife an offended look, then carried his daughter to the window.

"Look out there, sweetheart. That whole big world is yours. It's just waiting out there for you to take it by storm. You'll be the finest Ophelia who ever graced a stage. When you play Kate, you'll have the audience at your feet. And do you know who your biggest fan will be? Your daddy."

Baby Jennifer made squeaking, contented baby sounds, and Brick smiled at his wife as if he'd invented babies.

Helen smiled back. She thought perhaps he had.

Three years later . . .

Marsha tucked the letters she was going to mail into her handbag, then left her desk to peer into the bassinet. Baby Oliver lay on his stomach with his little rump in the air and his thumb in his mouth.

"Do you need anything else before morning, Helen?"

"No. Brick and I are taking the children to the park."

Marsha paused on her way out the door to lean over the bassinet and pat the plump little baby's bottom.

"The nanny is completely redundant. I don't know why you and Brick waste your money."

"We thought you needed help in trying to keep us straight."

"You've got that right. If you have any more babies, I'm going to have to ask for a raise. This job's getting too big for me to handle." Marsha's grin belied her words. She righted the hat she'd taken to wearing lately, then gave the baby one final pat. "See you in the morning, sweet pea."

Helen lifted her sleeping son from the bassinet and went to the nursery. John was on a little rocking horse with his baseball cap askew and his sneakers on the wrong feet. Brick sat in the middle of the floor, trying to fashion a bow of Jennifer's sash.

"You're letting her wear that frilly dress to the park?" Helen asked.

"She wanted to."

"She'll be much more comfortable in shorts."

"Ruffles, Mommy." Jennifer stuck out her little chin.

"She wants ruffles." Brick wore the look of a man totally besotted with his daughter.

Helen knew when she was outnumbered.

"Here. Hold the baby while I change John's shoes."

"No, Mommy," he said when she bent to put his shoes on the correct feet.

"He wanted to put on his shoes all by himself," Brick said.

"What am I going to do with you?" Helen said, smiling.

"Take me to the park?"

Brick, Helen, and baby Oliver lounged on a quilt under the shade of an oak tree while Jennifer and John romped in the sandbox nearby. John had both shoes off now, and was wiggling his feet in the sand while Jennifer raced around with a miniature dump truck making roaring noises. Her sash was untied, her dress was ripped, and her pink hair bow was perched rakishly over one ear.

Brick smiled at all his children, then reached for his wife's hand.

"I think we should reprise *The Taming of the Shrew*."

"I'm not ready to go back on the road."

"Who said anything about the road?" Brick turned Helen's hand over and kissed her palm. "How would you feel about starring right here in Atlanta at The Sullivan Theater."

"The Sullivan Theater?"

"We can build the kind of theater we've always wanted to play in, everything state of the art."

"It sounds wonderful."

"Just think, Helen. No more road trips. Total control of the plays we do. Onstage together whenever we want. Eventually we could bring a troupe in. The Sullivan Players."

Helen watched the twins frolicking about, screaming with laughter. Baby Oliver rolled over on his back and gave a big yawn before tumbling back into the baby dreams that occupied most of his day.

"We could have our own troupe," she said.

"Three is a good start."

"Four."

"Four?"

Smiling, Helen nodded. Brick stretched full length beside her and pressed his face against her abdomen.

"Hello in there, sweet little one. This is your daddy talking." He grinned up at Helen. "He didn't answer me."

"She."

"She?"

"I've decided to have another girl."

"The next time I get to choose the sex."

"Do you think there will be a next time?"

His grin was decidedly wicked as he pulled her down beside him on the quilt.

"My darling, I can guarantee it."

With the laughter of his children climbing toward the summer sun, Brick Sullivan went about the business of kissing his favorite leading lady.

YOU'VE READ THE BOOK.
NOW DOUBLE YOUR FUN BY ENTERING
LOVESWEPT'S TREASURED TALES III CONTEST!

Everybody loves a good romance, especially when that romance is inspired by a beloved fairy tale, legend, even a Shakespearean play. It's an entertaining challenge for the writer to create a contemporary retelling of a classic story—and for you, the reader, to find the similarities between the retold story and the classic.

For example:

- While reading STALKING THE GIANT by Victoria Leigh, did you notice that the heroine's nickname is exactly the same as the giant-slayer's in "Jack and the Beanstalk"?
- How about the fact that, like Adam and Eve, the hero and heroine in Glenna McReynold's DRAGON'S EDEN are alone in a paradise setting?
- Surely the heroine's red cape in HOT SOUTHERN NIGHTS by Patt Bucheister reminded you of the one Little Red Riding Hood wears on the way to her grandma's house.
- You couldn't have missed the heroine's rebuffing of the hero in Peggy Webb's CAN'T STOP LOVING YOU. Kate, in Shakespeare's *Taming of the Shrew*, displays the same steeliness when dealing with Petruchio.

The four TREASURED TALES III romances this month contain many, many more wonderful similarities to the classic stories they're based on. And with LOVESWEPT'S TREASURED TALES III CONTEST, you have a once-in-a-lifetime opportunity to let us know how many of these similarities you found. Even better, because this is LOVESWEPT's third year of publishing TREASURED TALES, this contest will have **three winners!**

Read the Official Rules to find out what you need to do to enter LOVESWEPT'S TREASURED TALES III CONTEST.

Now, indulge in the magic of TREASURED TALES III —and grab a chance to win some treasures of your own!

LOVESWEPT'S TREASURED TALES III CONTEST

OFFICIAL RULES:

1. *No purchase is necessary.* Enter by printing or typing your name, address, and telephone number at the top of one (or more, if necessary) piece(s) of 8½" X 11" plain white paper, if typed, or lined paper, if handwritten. Then list each of the similarities you found in one or more of the TREASURED TALES III romances to the classic story each is based on. The romances are STALKING THE GIANT by Victoria Leigh (based on "Jack and the Beanstalk"), DRAGON'S EDEN by Glenna McReynolds (based on "Adam and Eve"), HOT SOUTHERN NIGHTS by Patt Bucheister (based on "Little Red Riding Hood"), and CAN'T STOP LOVING YOU by Peggy Webb (based on *Taming of the Shrew*). Each book is available in libraries. Please be sure to list the similarities found below the title of the romance(s) read. Also, for use by the judges in case of a tie, write an essay of 150 words or less stating why you like to read LOVESWEPT romances. Once you've finished your list and your essay, mail your entry to: LOVESWEPT'S TREASURED TALES III CONTEST, Dept. BdG, Bantam Books, 1540 Broadway, New York, NY 10036.

2. PRIZES (3): All three (3) winners will receive a six (6) months' subscription to the LOVESWEPT Book Club and twenty-one (21) autographed books. Each winner will also be featured in a one-page profile that will appear in the back of Bantam Books' LOVESWEPT'S TREASURED TALES IV romances, scheduled for publication in February 1996. (Approximate retail value: $200.00)

3. Contest entries must be postmarked and received by March 31, 1995, and all entrants must be 21 or older on the date of entry. The author of each romance featured in LOVESWEPT'S TREASURED TALES III has provided a list of the similarities between her romance and the classic story it is based on. Entrants need not read all four TREASURED TALES III romances to enter, but the more they read, the more similarities they are likely to find. The entries submitted will be judged by members of the LOVESWEPT Editorial Staff, who will first count up the number of similarities each entrant identified, then compare the similarities found by the entrants who identified the most with the similarities listed by the author of the romance or romances read by those entrants and select the three entrants who correctly identified the greatest number of similarities. If more than three entrants correctly identify the greatest number, the judges will read the essays submitted by each potential winner in order to break the tie and select the entrants who submitted the best essays as the prize winners. The essays will be judged on the basis of the originality, creativity, thoughtfulness, and writing ability shown. All of the judges' decisions are final and binding. All essays must be original. Entries become the property of Bantam Books and will not be returned. Bantam Books is not responsible for incomplete or lost or misdirected entries.

4. Winners will be notified by mail on or about June 15, 1995. Winners have 30 days from the date of notice in which to claim their prize or an alternate winner will be chosen. Odds of winning are dependent on the number of entries received. Prizes are non-transferable and no substitutions are allowed. Winners may be required to execute an Affidavit Of Eligibility And Promotional Release supplied by Bantam Books and will need to supply a photograph of themselves for inclusion in the one-page profile of each winner. Entering the Contest constitutes permission for use of the winner's name, address (city and state), photograph, biographical profile, and Contest essay for publicity and promotional purposes, with no additional compensation.

5. Employees of Bantam Books, Bantam Doubleday Dell Publishing Group, Inc., their subsidiaries and affiliates, and their immediate family members are not eligible to enter. This Contest is open to residents of the U.S. and Canada, excluding the Province of Quebec, and is void wherever prohibited or restricted by law. Taxes, if any, are the winner's sole responsibility.

6. For a list of the winners, send a self-addressed, stamped envelope entirely separate from your entry to LOVESWEPT'S TREASURED TALES III CONTEST WINNERS LIST, Dept. BdG, Bantam Books, 1540 Broadway, New York, NY 10036. The list will be available after August 1, 1995.

THE EDITOR'S CORNER

   With March comes gray, rainy days and long, cold nights, but here at LOVESWEPT things are really heating up! The four terrific romances we have in store for you are full of emotion, humor, and passion, with sexy heroes and dazzling heroines you'll never forget. So get ready to treat yourself with next month's LOVESWEPTS—they'll definitely put you in the mood for spring.

   Starting things off is the delightfully unique Olivia Rupprecht with **PISTOL IN HIS POCKET**, LOVESWEPT #730. Lori Morgan might dare to believe in a miracle, that a man trapped for decades in a glacier can be revived, but she knows she has no business falling in love with the rough-hewn hunk! Yet when Noble Zhivago draws a breath in her bathtub, she feels reckless enough to respond to the dark stranger who seizes her lips and pulls her into the water. Wooed with passion and purpose by a magnificent warrior who tantalizes her senses, Lori must admit to adoring a man with a dangerous past. Olivia delivers both sizzling sensuality and heartbreaking emotion in this uninhibited romp.

The wonderfully talented Janis Reams Hudson's hero is **CAUGHT IN THE ACT**, LOVESWEPT #731. Betrayed, bleeding, and on the run, Trace Youngblood needs a hiding place—but will Lillian Roberts be his downfall, or his deliverance? The feisty teacher probably believes he is guilty as sin, but he needs her help to clear his name. Drawn to the rugged agent who embodies her secret yearnings, Lillian trusts him with her life, but is afraid she won't escape with her heart. Funny and wild, playful and explosive, smart and sexy, this is definitely another winner from Janis.

Rising star Donna Kauffman offers a captivating heart-stopper with **WILD RAIN**, LOVESWEPT #732. Jillian Bonner insists she isn't leaving, no matter how fierce the tempest headed her way, but Reese Braedon has a job to do—even if it means tossing the sweet spitfire over his shoulder and carrying her off! When the storm traps them together, the sparks that flash between them threaten spontaneous combustion. But once he brands her with the fire of his deepest need, she might never let him go. With a hero as wild and unpredictable as a hurricane, and a heroine who matches him in courage, will, and humor, Donna delivers a tale of outlaws who'd risk anything for passion—and each other.

Last, but never least, is the ever-popular Judy Gill with **SIREN SONG**, LOVESWEPT #733. Returning after fifteen years to the isolated beach where orca whales come to play, Don Jacobs once more feels seduced—by the place, and by memories of a young girl who'd offered him her innocence, a gift he'd hungered for but had to refuse. Tracy Maxwell still bewitches him, but is this beguiling woman of secrets finally free to surrender her heart? This evocative story explores the sweet mystery of longing and passion as only Judy Gill can.

Happy reading!

With warmest wishes,

Beth de Guzman

Senior Editor

P.S. Don't miss the women's novels coming your way in March: **NIGHT SINS**, the first Bantam hardcover by bestselling author Tami Hoag is an electrifying, heart-pounding tale of romantic suspense; **THE FOREVER TREE** by Rosanne Bittner is an epic, romantic saga of California and the courageous men and women who built their dreams out of redwood timber in the bestselling western tradition of Louis L'Amour; **MY GUARDIAN ANGEL** is an enchanting collection of romantic stories featuring a "guardian angel" theme from some of Bantam's finest romance authors, including Kay Hooper, Elizabeth Thornton, Susan Krinard, and Sandra Chastain; **PAGAN BRIDE** by Tamara Leigh is a wonderful historical romance in the bestselling tradition of Julie Garwood and Teresa Medeiros. We'll be giving you a sneak peek at these terrific books in next month's LOVESWEPTs. And immediately following this page, look for a preview of the exciting romances from Bantam that are *available now!*

Don't miss these irresistible books by
your favorite Bantam authors

On sale in January:

VALENTINE
by Jane Feather

*PRINCE OF
DREAMS*
by Susan Krinard

FIRST LOVES
by Jean Stone

From the beguiling, bestselling author of
Vixen and *Velvet* comes a tale brimming
with intrigue and passion

VALENTINE
BY
Jane Feather

"An author to treasure."
—*Romantic Times*

*A quirk of fate has made Sylvester Gilbraith the heir of his
sworn enemy, the earl of Stoneridge. But there's a catch: to
claim his inheritance he has to marry one of the earl's four
granddaughters. The magnetically handsome nobleman
has no choice but to comply with the terms of the will, yet
when he descends on Stoneridge Manor prepared to charm
his way into a fortune, he finds that the lady who intrigues
him most has no intention of becoming his bride. Maddeningly beautiful and utterly impossible, Theodora Belmont
refuses to admit to the chemistry between them, even when
she's passionately locked in his embrace. Yet soon the day
will come when the raven-haired vixen will give anything
to be Sylvester's bride and risk everything to defend his
honor . . . and his life.*

"You take one step closer, my lord, and you'll go
down those stairs on your back," Theo said. "And
with any luck you'll break your neck in the process."

Sylvester shook his head. "I don't deny your skill,
but mine is as good, and I have the advantage of size

and strength." He saw the acknowledgment leap into her eyes, but her position didn't change.

"Let's have done with this," he said sharply. "I'm prepared to forget that silly business by the stream."

"Oh, are you, my lord? How very generous of you. As I recall, you were not the one insulted."

"As I recall, you, cousin, were making game of me. Now, come downstairs. I wish you to ride around the estate with me."

"You wish me to do *what*?" Theo stared at him, her eyes incredulous.

"I understand from your mother that you've had the management of the estate for the last three years," he said impatiently, as if his request were the most natural imaginable. "You're the obvious person to show me around."

"You have windmills in your head, sir. I wouldn't give you the time of day!" Theo swung on her heel and made to continue up the stairs.

"You rag-mannered hoyden!" Sylvester exclaimed. "We may have started on the wrong foot, but there's no excuse for such incivility." He sprang after her, catching her around the waist.

She spun, one leg flashing in a high kick aimed at his chest, but as he'd warned her, this time he was ready for her. Twisting, he caught her body across his thighs, swinging a leg over hers, clamping them in a scissors grip between his knees.

"Now, yield!" he gritted through his teeth, adjusting his grip against the sinuous working of her muscles as she fought to free herself.

Theo went suddenly still, her body limp against him. Instinctively he relaxed his grip and the next instant she was free, bounding up the next flight of stairs.

Sylvester went after her, no longer capable of cool

reasoning. A primitive battle was raging and he knew only that he wasn't going to lose it. No matter that it was undignified and totally inappropriate.

Theo raced down the long corridor, hearing his booted feet pounding behind her in time with her thundering heart. She didn't know whether her heart was speeding with fear or exhilaration; she didn't seem capable of rational, coherent thought.

His breath was on the back of her neck as she wrenched open the door of her bedroom and leaped inside, but his foot went in the gap as she tried to slam the door shut. She leaned on the door with all her weight, but Sylvester put his shoulder against the outside and heaved. Theo went reeling into the room and the door swung wide.

Sylvester stepped inside, kicking the door shut behind him.

"Very well," Theo said breathlessly. "If you wish it, I'll apologize for being uncivil. I shouldn't have said what I did just now."

"For once we're in agreement," he remarked, coming toward her. Theo cast a wild look around the room. In a minute she was going to be backed up against the armoire and she didn't have too many tricks left.

Sylvester reached out and seized the long, thick rope of hair hanging down her back. He twisted it around his wrist, reeling her in like a fish until her face was on a level with his shoulder.

He examined her countenance as if he was seeing it for the first time. Her eyes had darkened and he could read the sparking challenge in their depths; a flush of exertion and emotion lay beneath the golden brown of her complexion and her lips were slightly parted, as if she was about to launch into another of her tirades.

To prevent such a thing, he tightened his grip on her plait, bringing her face hard against his shoulder, and kissed her.

Theo was so startled that she forgot about resistance for a split second, and in that second discovered that she was enjoying the sensation. Her lips parted beneath the probing thrust of his tongue and her own tongue touched his, at first tentatively, then with increasing confidence. She inhaled the scent of his skin, a sun-warmed earthy smell that was new to her. His mouth tasted of wine. His body was hard-muscled against her own, and when she stirred slightly she became startlingly aware of a stiffness in his loins. Instinctively she pressed her lower body against his.

Sylvester drew back abruptly, his eyes hooded as he looked down into her intent face. "I'll be damned," he muttered. "How many men have you kissed?"

"None," she said truthfully. Her anger had vanished completely, surprise and curiosity in its place. She wasn't even sure whether she still disliked him.

"I'll be damned," he said again, a slight smile tugging at the corners of his mouth, little glints of amusement sparking in the gray eyes. "I doubt you'll be a restful wife, cousin, but I'll lay odds you'll be full of surprises."

Theo remembered that she *did* dislike him . . . intensely. She twitched her plait out of his slackened grip and stepped back. "I fail to see what business that is of yours, Lord Stoneridge."

"Ah, yes, I was forgetting we haven't discussed this as yet," he said, folding his arms, regarding her with deepening amusement. "We're going to be married, you and I."

PRINCE OF DREAMS
BY
Susan Krinard

San Francisco psychologist Diana Ransom can't take her eyes off the gorgeous, green-eyed stranger. But when she finally approaches him across the smoke-filled room, her reasons have little to do with the treacherous feelings he inspires. Diana suspects that this brooding, enigmatic man is responsible for the disappearance of her young cousin. Desperate to find her, and determined to plumb the mystery behind Nicholas Gale's hypnotic charm, Diana will follow him into the velvety darkness . . . and awake to a haunting passion. For Nicholas is no mere human, but a vampire with the power to steal into a woman's dreams and fill her nights with untold rapture. And soon, blinded by an ecstasy sweeter than any she's ever known, Diana will find herself risking her eternal soul for a love that promises to be forever. . . .

For a moment the woman across the table was no more than a jumble of colors and heat and flaring life force. Nicholas struggled to focus on her face, on her stubborn, intelligent eyes.

He said the first thing that came into his head. "Do you have a first name, Dr. Ransom?"

She blinked at him, caught off guard and resentful of it. "I don't see what that has to do with Keely or where she is, Mr. Gale. That's all I'm interested in at the moment. If you—"

"Then we're back to where we started, Dr. Ransom. As it happens, I share your concern for Keely." He lost his train of thought for a moment, looking at the woman with her brittle control and overwhelming aura. He could almost hear the singing of her life force in the three feet of space between them.

He nearly reached out to touch her. Just to see what she would feel like, if that psychic energy would flow into him with so simple a joining.

He stopped his hand halfway across the table and clenched it carefully. She had never seen him move.

"What *is* your business, Mr. Gale?" she asked. The antagonism in her voice had grown muted, and there was a flicker of uncertainty in her eyes.

"I have many varied . . . interests," he said honestly. He smiled, and for a moment he loosed a tiny part of his hunter's power.

She stared at him and lifted a small hand to run her fingers through her short brown hair, effectively disordering the loose curls. That simple act affected Nicholas with unexpected power. He felt his groin tighten, a physical response he had learned to control and ignore long ago.

When was the last time? he asked himself. The last time he had lain with a woman, joined with her physically, taken some part of what he needed in the act of love?

Before he could blunt the thought, his imagination slipped its bonds, conjuring up an image of this woman, her aura ablaze, naked and willing and fully conscious beneath him. Knowing what he was, giving and receiving without fear. . . .

"Diana."

"What?" Reality ripped through Nicholas, dispelling the erotic, impossible vision.

"My first name is Diana," she murmured.

Her face was flushed, as if she had seen the lust in his eyes. She was an attractive woman. Mortal men would pursue her, even blind to her aura as they must be. Did she look at him and observe only another predictable male response to be dissected with an analyst's detachment?

His hungers were not so simple. He would have given the world to make them so.

"Diana," he repeated softly. "Huntress, and goddess of the moon."

She wet her lips. "It's getting late, Mr. Gale—"

"*My* first name is Nicholas."

"Nicholas," she echoed, as if by rote. "I'll be making a few more inquiries about Keely. If you were serious about being concerned for her—"

"I was."

Diana twisted around in her chair and lifted a small, neat purse. "Here," she said, slipping a card from a silver case. "This is where you can reach me if you should hear from her."

Nicholas took the card and examined the utilitarian printing. *Diana Ransom, Ph.D. Licensed Psychologist. Individual psychotherapy. Treatment of depression, anxiety, phobias, and related sleep disorders.*

Sleep disorders. Nicholas almost smiled at the irony of it. She could never cure his particular disorder. He looked up at her. "If you need to talk to me again, I'm here most nights."

"Then you don't plan to leave town in the next few days?" she asked with a touch of her former hostility.

His gaze was steady. "No, Diana. I'll make a few inquiries of my own."

They stared at each other. *Diana.* Was she a child of the night, as her name implied? Did she dream vivid dreams that he could enter as he could never enter her body? Or was she part of the sane and solid world of daylight, oblivious to the untapped power that sang in her aura like a beacon in darkness?

She was the first to look away. Hitching the strap of her purse higher on her shoulder, she rose. "Then I'll be going." She hesitated, slanting a look back at him with narrowed blue eyes. "Perhaps we'll see each other again . . . Nicholas."

He watched her walk away and up the stairs. Her words had held a warning. No promise, no hint of flirtation. With even a little effort he could have won her over. He could have learned more about her, perhaps enough to determine if she would be a suitable candidate to serve his needs. One glimpse of her aura was enough to tempt him almost beyond reason.

But she had affected him too deeply. He could not afford even the slightest loss of control with his dreamers. Emotional detachment was a matter of survival—his and that of the women he touched by night.

Diana Ransom was something almost beyond his experience—.

Although he would never sample the promise behind Diana Ransom's unremarkable façade, would never slip into her dreams and skim the abundance of energy that burned beneath her skin. . . .

As he had done a thousand times before, Nicholas schooled himself to detachment and consigned hope and memory to their familiar prisons. If he arranged matters correctly, he need never see Diana Ransom again.

What if you could go back and rediscover
the magic . . . ?

FIRST LOVES
BY
Jean Stone

*For every woman there is a first love, the love she never
forgets. You always wonder what would have happened,
what might have been. Here is a novel of three women
with the courage to go back . . . but could they recover
the magic they left behind?*

"Men," Alissa said. "They really are scum, you
know."

"Maybe it's partly our fault," Meg replied quietly.

"Are you nuts?" Alissa asked. "Besides, how
would you know? You're not even married." She took
a sip of wine. "Bet you have a boyfriend, though.
Some equally successful power attorney, perhaps? Or
maybe that private investigator? What was his
name?"

"His name is Danny. And no, he's only a friend. A
good friend. But right now, there's no one special in
my life."

Alissa set down her glass. "See? If someone as
beautiful and clever and smart as you doesn't have a
boyfriend, it proves they're all scum. I rest my case."

Though she knew Alissa's words could be considered a compliment, Meg suddenly found old feelings
resurfacing, the feelings of being the kid with no fa-

ther, the one who was different, inadequate. "I've had a lot of boyfriends—men friends," she stuttered.

"But how about relationships?" Alissa pressed. "*Real* relationships?"

In her mind Meg saw his face, his eyes, his lips. She felt his touch. "Once," she replied quietly, "a long time ago."

Alissa leaned back in her chair. "Yeah, I guess you could say I had one once, too. But it sure as shit wasn't with my husband. It was before him." She drained her glass and poured another. "God, it was good."

Meg was relieved to have the focus of the conversation off herself. "What happened?"

"His name was Jay. Jay Stockwell. Our parents had summer homes next to each other."

"You were childhood sweethearts?" Zoe asked, then added wistfully, "I think they're the best. Everyone involved is so innocent."

Alissa shook her head. "This wasn't innocence. It was love. Real love."

They grew quiet. Meg thought of Steven Riley, about their affair. That was love. Real love. But it was years ago. A lifetime ago.

The waiter arrived and set their dinners on the red paper placemats. Meg stared at the cheeseburger. Suddenly she had no appetite.

After he left, Zoe spoke. "What is real love, anyway? How do you know? William took good care of me and of Scott. But I can't honestly say I loved him. Not like I'd loved the boy back home."

"Ah," Alissa said, "the boy back home. For me, that was Jay. The trouble was, he didn't want to stay home. He had things to do, a world to save."

"Where did he go?"

Meg was glad Zoe was keeping Alissa talking. She

could feel herself sliding into the lonely depression of thoughts of Steven. She could feel her walls closing around her, her need to escape into herself. For some reason she thought about the cat she'd had then—a gray tiger named Socrates. For the longest time after Steven was gone she'd closed Socrates out of her bedroom. She'd not been able to stand hearing him purr; the sound was too close to the soft snores of Steven beside her, at peace in his slumber after their lovemaking.

"First, Jay went to San Francisco," Alissa was saying, and Meg snapped back to the present. "It was in the early seventies. He'd been deferred from the draft. From Vietnam."

"Was he sick?" Zoe asked.

"No," Alissa said. "He was rich. Rich boys didn't have to go. Jay's family owned—and still do—a mega-broadcast conglomerate. TV stations. Radio stations. All over the country. Jay loved broadcasting, but not business. He was a born journalist." She pushed the plate with her untouched cheeseburger and fries aside. "When he went to San Francisco, he gave his family the finger."

"And you never saw him again?" Zoe asked.

Alissa laughed. "Never saw him again? Darling," she said, as she took another sip of wine, "I went with him."

"You went with him?" Even Meg was surprised at this. She couldn't picture Alissa following anyone, anywhere.

"I was eighteen. Love seemed more important than trust funds or appearances or social standing."

"So what happened?" Zoe asked.

She shrugged. "I realized I was wrong."

The women were quiet. Meg felt sorry for Alissa. Something in the eyes of this tiny, busy, aggressive little blonde now spelled sorrow. Sorrow for a life gone by. Sorrow for love relinquished. She knew the feeling only too well.

"God, he was handsome," Alissa said. "He still is."

"Still is?" Zoe asked. "You mean you still see him?"

Alissa shook her head. "I left him standing at the corner of Haight and Ashbury. It seemed appropriate at the time. He was working for one of those liberal underground newspapers. I went home to Atlanta, married Robert, had the kids. Then one day I turned on the TV and there he was. Reporting from Cairo."

"So he went back into broadcasting," Zoe said.

"Full steam ahead, apparently. Delivering stories on the oppressed peoples of the world. Over the years I've seen him standing against backdrops in Lebanon, Ethiopia, Iraq, you name it. He was on the air for days during that Tiananmen Square thing in China or wherever that is."

"Oh," Zoe said, "Jay Stockwell. Sure. I've seen him, too. His stories have real sensitivity."

Alissa shrugged. "I never paid much attention to his stories. I was too busy looking at him. Wondering."

Zoe picked at her scallops, then set down her fork. "Wondering what would have happened if you'd stayed together?"

"Sure. Haven't you ever done that? Wondered about your boy back home?"

"You mean, the man I could have married?" Zoe asked.

"Or should have," Alissa said.

Should have, Meg thought. Should I have? Could I have?

"Sure I've wondered about him," Zoe said. "All the time."

"What about you, Meg? What about your one and only? Don't you ever wonder how your life would have been different. How it would have been better?"

Meg silently wished she could say, "No. My life wouldn't have been better. It would have been worse. And besides, my life is just fine the way it is." But she couldn't seem to say anything. She couldn't seem to lie.

There was silence around the table. Meg looked at Zoe, who was watching Alissa. Meg turned to Alissa, just in time to see her quickly wipe a lone tear from her cheek. Alissa caught Meg's eye and quickly cleared her throat. Then she raised her glass toward them both. "I think we should find them," Alissa said. "I think we should find the men we once loved, and show them what they've missed."

And don't miss these fabulous romances
from Bantam Books,
on sale in February:

NIGHT SINS
Available in hardcover
by the nationally bestselling author

Tami Hoag

THE FOREVER TREE
by the award-winning

Rosanne Bittner

PAGAN BRIDE
by the highly acclaimed

Tamara Leigh

"MY GUARDIAN ANGEL"
anthology featuring:

Sandra Chastain   Kay Hooper
Susan Krinard   Karyn Monk
Elizabeth Thornton